# The Providence of Basketball

Rick Collins

ISBN: 9781076364500

# DEDICATION

*To Marcus, wherever you are.*

Rick Collins

# CONTENTS

# ACKNOWLEDGMENTS

This story has been in my mind for a very long time. I want to thank my grandparents: Armand and Concorde Beaumont, and Ed and Ruth Collins. My summers as a kid would not have been the same without their love. I want to thank my wife, Betsy, for all of her encouragement, especially when I thought I might give up on this story. I want to thank Vangella Buchanan of The Writery Ink, LLC. She inspired me to write this story because she understood how little I knew about anything and had the kindness to help me figure things out. Finally, I want to thank Marcus, wherever he is today, for walking me home from the basketball court on Cranston Street on that hot night in Providence 44 years ago.

Rick Collins

# Chapter 1

## Dumps and Ball Fields

I climbed in the big-ass Ford Fairlane my dad let me drive when he wasn't doing coach stuff around town. I started the engine and turned on the old AM radio because we couldn't afford a tape deck. Ozzy Osborne screamed from the speakers. The guitar hammered and I threw the car in reverse and backed out of my driveway without looking back. My dad yells at me for driving like a madman, but I haven't hit anyone yet, so right now, I still don't care. I drove through my hometown of West Beaumont, Massachusetts, past the old dump that the town covered over with tons of sand and planted grass to make ball fields. Deep under the turf and dirt, there are old shaving cream containers from the Gillette plant down the road and left-over chemicals from Raytheon where they built Patriot Missiles. Incredulously, the town decided to turn the old toxic waste site into a bunch of baseball fields and soccer pitches. Teams played long games there under the summer sky and darkness, illuminated flatteringly by flood lights. I drove by and shook my head thinking about how people think things are a certain way when clearly, they are not. Perhaps this wasn't my town's best idea.

I drove past the elementary school where I used to play youth football and then past the old, gothic cemetery where I kissed my first girlfriend. I drove to the high school with its silent, stone façade. The town built it years ago when the population of West Beaumont burst at the seams. It had the architectural creativity of a maximum-security prison. The building had no air conditioning, so every day in class, we would sweat until our butts stuck to the cheap plastic chairs with the steel frames underneath where we could stick our books that we hardly ever opened. The outdoor basketball court at the high school, the one with the perfect twine nets, was right next to this big hill with an ancient rock that the kids in town painted over just about every night with messages like "Give Peace a Chance" or "Mary Lou and Mike TLF," or "Go Climb a Rock." I parked my car and slid out of the front seat and put on my Converse All-Star high cut perfectly-white basketball shoes that I only wore when my buddies and I would run all night, as long as no one knocked the flood lights out with rocks. That kind of thing didn't usually happen in West Beaumont.

My best friends, James and Michael and Joe and Kahlil and I took on any team who thought they could beat us in hoop. James and Michael and Joe played on the varsity basketball team, and Kahlil and I ran indoor track. I used to play basketball every waking hour before I turned sixteen when I realized that, even though I was good, I was still 5'8" and had stopped growing when I was fourteen and I probably wasn't going to play college basketball. But I could still play pretty well, and I could definitely run and so could Kahlil, so the five of us played all night all summer and beat just about everyone who took us on.

James and Michael were my best friends since I was just a kid. James lived up the street from me, across from this old pine forest where we used to build forts and race our bikes until we crashed into one of the pine trees. I met James on a sticky summer's day when we were having pine cone wars where we'd pick up these really big pine cones and pelt each other. James and his sister Cecille were on one team and I was on the other team with a bunch of my other buddies from the neighborhood. James's team charged and we thought we'd held them off and protected our part of the pine forest when out of nowhere, I'm flat on the ground after being hit in the head with a rock. James stood about twenty feet away and he laughed at me thinking it was funny because kids hit each other with rocks back then. I think his sister probably was smarter than James and me because she saw the look in my eyes like I was going to flatten James, so she ran and then James saw me get up and chase him, so he ran out of the pine forest and across the street to his house where he could run inside under the false pretense of safety. Of course, I didn't care about that, because you know, he hit me in the head with a rock, so I grabbed the door knob and flung it open and busted inside.

James's mom was there, and James was clearly shocked that this maniac kid just crashed through the front door about to punch him on the nose. She held up her hands like she thought I would stop, so I did because James's mom was, you know, a mom and kids didn't mess with moms back then like the way they do today. She asked me why I was so mad, and James said I was crazy, and I said no, that he hit me in the head with a rock. Cecille said her brother didn't mean it, so I began to calm down a bit.

From behind James's mom, a man stood up. He wore this hat with a felt band that wrapped around it. The hat looked like the kind someone would wear if his name was Luigi or Fredo. It was James's dad. He had a dark complexion and he wore thick, opaque glasses that looked like the bottom of a Coke bottle. He asked me what my name was, so I told him. He said that he was sure his son did in fact hit me in the head with a rock because he knew his son was stupid so I shouldn't hold it against him. He said that maybe I should sit down with him at the kitchen table and he told James and Cecille to sit down too, and he began to tell us a story about a time when he and his brother got in a fight and they punched each other in the eye and then forgot about it within a few minutes because they both wanted to go swim in a pond near where they grew up. I figured he was trying to get me to forget that his son hit me in the head with a rock, and I saw no reason to argue because by then, James's mom brought out cookies, and nothing ends a fight like two kids eating cookies. So we sat at the kitchen table and James's dad and mom told us stories all afternoon about when they grew up, and I saw how much they loved each other and I knew that James was going to be a friend of mine forever, even though I had sticky blood on my scalp from, you know, the rock.

I found out later that James's dad had eye surgery and that's why he wore those thick glasses and that he was just about blind, but I didn't care because James's dad was kind to me and very smart and he was a lawyer and I had never met a lawyer before. I liked him right away since he knew his son was stupid for hitting me in the head with a rock.

I met Michael a few years later when he and his family moved in from Long Island, which to me was a completely different country because no one in his family liked the Red Sox. I met him when he was trying out for the West Beaumont Charger youth football team. He almost beat me in a wind sprint during tryouts, so naturally, I wanted to meet him. I walked the mile from my house to his house to introduce myself. He wasn't home when I knocked on the glass door of his walk-in living room, so I waited around until his mom drove up their long, hilly driveway that I thought was weird because you couldn't play street hockey on a hilly driveway, so why buy a house like that anyway?

Michael's mom parked the car at the top. She stepped out of the car and I thought she was really pretty, kind of like models were really pretty. Michael and his brother Mark and their little sister Paula hopped out of the car and Michael and Mark were wearing matching green New York Jets letter jackets with the long white arms that were made of something that looked like the slippery material of a couch we had in my living room. Both Michael and Mark carried big cases that I found out later were for trumpets, which I thought was odd, because in the Catholic school I went to, they didn't teach anyone how to play instruments except the girls who they taught how to play guitar, but for some reason didn't let the boys learn how to play. That always pissed me off.

Anyway, when Michael saw me sitting on the back deck of his house, he didn't recognize me at first. I told him my name and that remember, we met at football tryouts yesterday, and I think he pretended like he remembered, but that didn't matter to me because he was now my friend, as far as I was concerned. He asked me if I wanted to come in and I said yes and his mom asked if I wanted cookies, so you know, they were cookies, so I said yes, and she asked Paula to get some out of the cupboard. I thought they would be Oreos or Fig Newtons or something like the cookies everyone ate, but they were these fancy Long Island

Italian cookies that I had never seen before. I said thanks because my dad made sure I always said thanks, and I took a bite of one of the cookies and I thought it was pretty good, but they weren't like the Oreos my dad and me put in this big red apple ceramic thing that was what we used for a cookie jar.

Michael and Mark and Paula and me sat on the white couch in their living room that I swear was the same material as the arms on their New York Jets football jackets. I sat on the end of the couch and I kept slipping off because the couch was brand new and was slippery as a new skillet. Michael put on "The Three Stooges" and we laughed like we had been friends forever, like kids can do without being taught how to do it.

# Chapter 2

## White or Black

I met Joe when my dad took me to this dinner for black kids who came to our town from around the country to go to high school. The program was called "ABC" for "A Better Chance." My dad was on the national board of directors and our town had been one of the first towns to offer scholarships to black kids from tough situations like deep in the city or poor, rural farm communities. The dinner was at the house where the black kids lived during the school year. It had this really big room where a bunch of people could eat. I thought it might have been a church before it housed the black kids. I sat with my dad and they served this wicked thick meatloaf with way too many spices, probably to disguise whatever kind of meat they used. I smothered it with cheap ketchup, not Heinz, but the cheap stuff you can buy from those big supermarkets. And I ate it because, you know, it was meatloaf and I liked meatloaf.

Across from me was this skinny kid with a long face and an easy smile. I told him my name was Tim and he told me his name was Joe and he was from Hotlanta. I said I had never heard of Hotlanta and he laughed this deep throated laugh that kind of surprised me since he was so skinny. He told me it was "Hotlanta" as in Atlanta because it's always hot down where he lived. This made me laugh and I kind of burped some of the meatloaf that I ate too fast, and he laughed at me and it never occurred to me that I should be upset with a black kid laughing at me.

I find it kind of interesting, that somehow food seems to be the one thing that was the common denominator for meeting all my friends. Cookies and meatloaf. Who knew?

Kahlil was the last of my four friends that I got to know. He wasn't that tall, but he had this sick afro that made him look about six foot one. I met him when we had our first practice together at indoor track. He had this really long stride for a kid who was my height, and I had this choppy, whack, whack, whack stride that was about two to everyone one of his. I guess my hips kind of waddled when I ran, at least that was what Kahlil said in the locker room after practice. I was fast, and it was obvious he was just as fast, if not faster, and I thought we were going to be rivals at first, but after he made fun of my waddling, I told him he looked like a tree and he laughed at me and said, "Damn," and I laughed and said, "What do you think I am, a duck?" and he said, "Ya, a damn duck," and that made me howl and my friends called me the damn duck from then on.

Kahlil's real home was in this place called Co-Op City in Brooklyn. I told him I had never heard of Co-Op City, and he said he wasn't surprised because I was the first white person he had ever had a conversation with, so of course I figured Co-Op City was probably not the best place to grow up. He told me he lived in a building that had five thousand people in it. I said he had to be crazy, and he said that I had never been there so how would I know. I still thought he was nuts, but I didn't want to push it because we were just new friends and what did I know about living in a city anyway, coming from the sticks of West Beaumont where there just weren't that many black kids in town? Actually, I think when Joe and Kahlil moved to our school, that brought the number up to about ten. But I was getting to know Joe and Kahlil and they were black, so I figured every black kid had to be just like them. I told Kahlil I would have to go visit him sometime when he was back home in Co-Op City. He said that maybe that wasn't the best idea.

So, I finished tying my perfectly white, high-top Converse All-Stars and ran on the court and yelled, "We got next!" which means we get to play the next game against the team that just won. A bunch of older white kids from some different town had been winning for a while and they looked like they thought they were going to beat us, too. We got on the court and one of their guys threw a pass and I picked it off and raced to the basket on the other end of the court. I gathered myself like I was going to spring up for a layup and this big guy from the other team, who was pissed that I picked off his pass, chased me like he was going to swat my layup out of the court and across the street to where my car was parked. I guess I knew he was about to swat my shot, so just as I was about to do my layup, I bounced the ball backwards between my legs to Joe who was chasing behind. The older white kid crashed into me and we went sprawling out of bounds and I skinned my elbows on the smooth, beige colored concrete.

Meanwhile, Joe gathered up my pass and drove his knee into the air and exploded up, and with two hands, dunked the ball and hung on the rim and let out a yell like they do when they dunk in Atlanta. Michael and James and Kahlil whooped in triumph and pointed at Joe like you do when someone does something great playing basketball. I jumped up and gave the older white kid a little tap on his butt like, "Hey, nice try," and he was pissed even more and so were his buddies. It didn't matter though, because James rained jump shots and Michael leaped for rebound after rebound, and Joe kept dunking on them, and I kept stealing the ball and passing down court so Kahlil could score because he was seriously fast and no one could catch him. We kicked the crap out of the older white kids from wherever they came from. When it was over, those guys reluctantly fist-bumped us, and they were so pissed, they got in their old car and left, tires squealing in defeat.

That was fine with me because they were bigger than us and could probably kill us in a fight, but I knew at least they couldn't beat us in hoop. Ever. I yelled out, "Who's next?" and another team got on the court and we busted them too and everyone else that night until it got so late the timer on the six flood lights that surrounded our court finally went off and it became wicked dark. We walked over to where my big ass Ford Fairlane waited in the parking lot and we pulled out water or soda or I think Michael pulled out a beer from a cooler he brought and we hung out in the deep of the night and talked crap about how good we were at basketball, like young dudes do when they think they are all that and a bag of chips.

As we hung out in the dark, I told my buddies that I was off to spend a week in Providence, Rhode Island with my French-Canadian grandparents so I wouldn't be able to play basketball with them next week. Michael said, "Providence?" like it was something bad. I said that I was going to Providence and what was the big deal, and James jumped in and said that he had never been to Providence. He kind of laughed when he said it, like he would never go to a place like Providence. Kahlil and Joe knew that it was some city in Rhode Island, but they kind of laughed when they said the word "city" because, you know, Atlanta and Brooklyn were actual, big cities.

"Where in Providence?" Kahlil looked at me kind of sideways.

"My grandparents live near the Cranston Street Armory. Right in the middle of the city."

Joe turned and looked right at me.

"In the middle of the city. Really."

"Yeah, really, so what?"

"You been there before?"

Kahlil kept his sideways glance as he sucked down a Coke.

"Yeah, I've been there before. They're my grandparents."

"Well, you damn duck, what kind of neighborhood do they live in? White? Black? What?"

Now Kahlil turned and looked right at me. I could see his bright eyes staring at me though the dark.

"They're white, so I guess a white neighborhood, but to be honest, I don't really know since I haven't been there in a while."

Now James stopped drinking from his water bottle and looked at me and Michael finished his beer and looked at me and I saw that

Kahlil and Joe were also staring at me like maybe I was a dope or something.

"Isn't Providence mostly black?" Michael kind of laughed when he said it.

"I think it is mostly black," Joe jumped in. "What are you going to do for a week in a city that's mostly black that surrounds your grandparent's house?"

Now that I thought about it, the last time my dad and I visited my grandparents in Providence, he had locked the doors to our car when we turned past the Cranston Street Armory and drove down the street past a whole bunch of duplex houses with black people on the porch or hanging out of windows or walking on the street or just standing on a corner. At the time, I didn't think about it much, but my dad got really quiet when we got off the highway and drove near the Armory.

"So what?" I said and I was being a dope. "They have a park across the street. They got basketball courts. I'll shoot hoops by myself or jump in some games. What are they going to do to me?"

Now, I really did sound like a dope, but I was sixteen and I was immortal and what could possibly go wrong?

Kahlil got up off the ground where he was stretching out his seriously long legs and he put his hand on my shoulder like he knew stuff I didn't.

"Sure. You'll be fine. I'm sure the brothers will be quite happy to allow you to participate."

Kahlil had this way of using a perfectly white sounding voice when he wanted to make fun of me.

"Well, I'm leaving tomorrow. It's like you think you'll never see me again. It's just Providence."

"Tell us how it goes *if* you get back."

Michael laughed at me and so did James and Joe and Kahlil, so I told them to shut the hell up.

# Chapter 3

## Little Rhody

That Sunday, my dad and me packed into our old, rusted station wagon with the one tire that was always under-inflated, and we got onto Route 93 South through Reading and Woburn and then took a right onto Route 128 near Boston and joined the heavy traffic and crept along until, finally, we headed south onto Route 95 and across the border past Attleboro into Pawtucket, Rhode Island. Since the state is so small, too quickly we could see the outline, such as it is, of the capital of the Ocean State, Providence, Rhode Island.

Rhode Island is the smallest state in the country. It seemed to me, and what did I know, that maybe Massachusetts and Connecticut had this piece of land stuck between them that they didn't know what to do with, so they shrugged their shoulders and said Rhode Island was on its own. I read somewhere that it was actually this guy named Roger Williams who was sick of Massachusetts, so he packed up his gear and his family and friends and headed south and invented Rhode Island. I think I leaned that in a history class.

My mom and dad grew up in Rhode Island. My dad grew up in East Providence. His father worked for a steel company after he came home from the war in the Pacific. He was a medic who somehow physically survived some of the worst battles of the war, but he never really left them behind. His life was hard, and he had his demons and he ended up losing both of his legs to diabetes when I was just a little kid. My dad's mom was a spitfire who probably was the only person in the world who could love and live with my dad's dad, but she loved her husband and never left him, and she adored her only son.

My dad told me that my mom's parents grew up in Quebec and moved to Fall River for work right after World War II. They emigrated from Fall River and moved into Providence with a whole bunch of other French-Canadian speaking families, and they made the center of Providence their own. My mom's dad was a tool maker when he moved his family to Providence, back when there were still plenty of manufacturing jobs. My mom's mom worked as a seamstress for the Italian families who also moved into Providence on the north side of the city around the same time. They both worked long hours all their lives, even up to the time when they were in their seventies when I decided that I wanted to spend a week with them.

Providence had its ethnic neighborhoods like just every city. The Irish lived over by the east side of the city near Brown University and the Italians lived on the north side and the Portuguese lived on the south side and the French-Canadians lived right smack in the center of Providence. So that made for an interesting stew of humanity. Then, after World War II, when the soldiers came home and wanted to start families and get jobs and begin peaceful lives, the government and the banks started giving out G.I. loans. Men could use the loans for college or to buy houses and get married and have kids and go to good schools. The only little issue was that the G.I. loans were mostly for the white soldiers and not the black ones.

Then the banks and local towns and cities decided to designate parts of cities and towns with certain colors, like green lines for white people who could get loans for this white part of town, or yellow lines for maybe where white people shouldn't buy a house because black people might want to live there too, or red lines where banks told white people to move out or don't buy a house there because this is where the black people lived and you certainly don't want a house where the black people lived. It was all about property values, of course, to the governments and the banks.

It was just business, with just a touch of poverty thrown in, because a man's value is defined by the house where he lives, at least to the people handing out the money, and since black people couldn't get loans, they got stuck renting apartments or old houses in the deep parts of cities where the red lines were drawn. Most wealth in America is defined by property. If a family could own a home, they could build up equity and use that equity to send their kids to college or sell the home and move to a place where there might be better schools, thereby breaking the cycle of poverty. Pretty easy for white soldiers when the government was eager to loan them cheap money. Almost impossible when the government made systemic decisions to purposefully keep loans out of the hands of black soldiers.

Redlining made it almost impossible for black families to buy homes and create wealth. Nice. Some civic leaders felt a little guilty, so they decided to start these building projects where the black folk could find decent places to live, but the building projects didn't quite work out that way because the bums who owned the "projects" charged just enough so the black folk could live there, but never kept up the projects so they soon fell into disrepair. Of course, once the black folk moved into the projects, the manufacturing jobs moved away to where the white people lived who were willing to work for cheap wages or where the taxes were low so they could make money, so that wasn't so good for black families. Providence did this too, especially in the deep, hot, red-lined part of the city near the Cranston Street Armory where my mom's parents still lived.

Now, both my sets of grandparents were loving, kind, considerate, and most definitely stubborn people. My Poppy, my mom's dad, refused to move out of his Providence neighborhood when the rest of the white people fled the black people, because, you see, this was his neighborhood and he was damned if anyone was going to make him leave. After the neighborhood turned mostly black, he couldn't have left anyway because the value of his house had depreciated. That's what happens to all-black neighborhoods.

Poppy's house was one of two, two-story duplexes on Cranston Street that still had white people in it. His neighbor in the other white duplex was this guy named Jean Beauchamp, but my Poppy just called him Beauchamp. My Poppy didn't like him very much, and so he called him "That damn Beauchamp" this or "That damn Beauchamp" that. They'd swear at each other in French-Canadian all day unless something interrupted them, like a ball game on the radio or Beauchamp getting up from his chair and going inside his duplex, slamming the door behind him because it got too loud and crazy on Cranston Street. My Poppy would come back into his apartment in his duplex and my Meme would try to calm him down. It usually took a couple hours and some Narragansett Beer, but he'd settle down and then turn on his tiny, 1960s vintage radio and sit and listen to the Red Sox game with a French-Canadian announcer.

On Sunday afternoon, we pulled in front of my Poppy and Meme's duplex when the temperature in Providence was so hot the tires on our old, rusted station wagon had gooey tar stuck in the treads from the melting pavement. Jean Beauchamp was sprawled out on his old rocking chair on the porch of his duplex next door. He read the Providence Journal newspaper, and without looking up yelled out, "Bon jour" in this sour kind of voice like the pollution from Providence had done a job on his vocal chords. My dad and me yelled back, "Bon jour" and then he ignored us, so we tried to ignore him.

My Poppy and Meme came out of their apartment onto their porch with the two rocking chairs and the fading grey paint. My dad and my Poppy shook hands manfully. They made eye contact like men do. My dad then gave my Meme a long hug. After my mom left when I was three, Meme and Poppy stayed in touch and came to visit in the summer and made sure to let me know how much they loved me. It had to be hard for them knowing that their daughter had left a husband and little boy. Whatever guilt they felt, they kept it to themselves when they came to visit us or we spent a few hours with them in Providence.

After having lunch and talking about how jobs were leaving Providence and all of the problems that were going on between black families and the cops and how sometimes the National

Guard patrolled the streets to help keep the peace, my dad decided it was time for him to go. I had one suitcase filled with random clothes and my perfectly white high-top basketball shoes buried deep in a gym bag and an old, red, white, and blue ABA basketball with the Julius Irving mock autograph handwritten on a white panel of the ball. I kissed my dad goodbye. He hugged my Meme warmly and thanked her for a wonderful afternoon. He shook my Poppy's hand and turned to me and said, "Be a good boy."

My dad walked down the porch steps and put the key into the lock of the old rusted station wagon. He turned on the car and it coughed and gagged, but eventually came to life. I noticed as he drove away that he locked the front door to the station wagon. Our car turned into traffic and my dad made a U-turn in front of a liquor store on the corner and came back around and drove past my Meme and Poppy's duplex. I waved at him from the front porch and watched him drive away, passed the assorted black people walking on the sidewalk or talking on their porches or hanging on the street corner.

I looked out into the blaze of the late afternoon in Providence and I could see steaming waves of heat shimmer off Cranston Street and the parking lot to the armory. Across the street, there was a noisy park where winos hung out and drank from bottles in paper bags and music blared from boom boxes carried on young men's shoulders, and guys with no shirts ran up and down two basketball courts on the far side of the park about a quarter mile away. I thought to myself that that looked like fun and that after my grandparents' French-Canadian dinner of fried fish and French fries with mustard and vinegar, I would grab my gym bag and my red, white, and blue ABA ball with the Julius Irving mock autograph and run across Cranston Street to see if I was good enough to play with the black guys.

# Chapter 4

## Juice

It was about seven at night when I helped clean up dinner with my Poppy and Meme. Poppy asked me if I wanted to listen to the Red Sox with him on the radio. He had a little transistor radio he said I could use by putting it up to my ear and listening to the Red Sox on the English station, only if I kept it way down so he wouldn't have to strain to hear the French-Canadian broadcaster from the French-Canadian station. I told him I would catch the game later on because I wanted to play basketball in the park.

"You're not playing over there, Timothy. You stay here with us."

"Poppy, I'm just playing basketball."

"It's not safe, especially at night. Do you hear the noises from outside?"

I did hear lots of summer-time city noises like roaring engines and loud voices passing in front of my grandparents' duplex and Marvin Gaye music from stereos stuck outside the windows of the black folk's apartments in the projects that surrounded Cranston Street. I also heard way off in the distance the unmistakable sound of a basketball pounding into the pavement of outdoor courts.

"He's a big boy now, so let him go, Poppy." My grandmother called her husband "Poppy" anytime I was at their house. "He'll be fine. And if he dies, we'll know soon enough, because he'll die right across the park."

I thought that wasn't so reassuring, but I was glad my Meme took my side of the argument because it was hard to argue with a grandfather, especially a French-Canadian grandfather.

"I'll be fine, really, Poppy. If I get killed, I'll be sure to let you know immediately," I laughed and grabbed my gym bag with my hoop gear and my ABA basketball, and I opened their front door and ran out onto the porch and into the early evening dusk that started to darken Providence.

Just as I was about to jump off the porch, Jean Beauchamp came out and smoked a fat cigar and sat on his rocking chair on the porch of his duplex. It was separated by about six feet from my grandparents' duplex so he could just about spit on me if he wanted to, and it looked like he wanted to.

"You planning on playing with the coloreds? They'll kill you, if I know coloreds, and I know coloreds."

He pulled his cigar out from his teeth and spit out a stream of tobacco juice that sailed off his porch and landed by the feet of this old black lady and this little black girl who were walking by right at that moment. They saw the tobacco juice flying so they jumped out of the way before it splattered against the simmering concrete and stained their legs.

"Watch out for the tobacco juice!" he laughed, and the old black lady and little black girl hurried off, but not before the old black lady told Beauchamp he was an old cracker.

"I'll spit where I damn well please. You coloreds watch where you walk," he snickered, and even in the early summer night I could see big, green, tobacco-stained rotten teeth in the hole of his face.

"What are you looking at?"

He spat more tobacco as he saw me watching the disgusting scene. This time when he tried to spit, the juice caught against his revolting teeth, and instead of flying out like snake venom, it dribbled off his bottom lip and drooled onto his old, wife beater t-shirt. He swore and used his hand to wipe off the repulsive liquid, but only managed to grind in the juice with the many stains that already resided on his shirt. He put his old cigar back in the hole in his face and the cigar was dead, so he lit it and he blew out a thin line of smoke, like some dying dragon.

I laughed at him loud enough that I was sure he could hear me.

His eyes narrowed and more blue smoke escaped from between his rotten teeth, so I knew I bothered him. Part of me was very pleased about that.

I picked up my ball and my gym bag and ran across the pavement of the road, just before a hot rod blaring music charged down Cranston Street. It missed me by about two feet as I bounded across the street and made a direct line toward the basketball courts. There were groups of black men and black women and black children eating barbeque on a picnic table near an old, outdoor grill that was built into the park. I walked by them with this cocky kind of saunter and the black people stopped eating and stared at me without saying a word as I dribbled my ABA ball on the dirt of the park. Each time the ball hit the ground, a little vortex of dust would spiral up. Up to that point, my Poppy and Meme's neighborhood was just some old, framed picture to me and not a pulsing, living, breathing world. But when the black people stopped eating and looked up from their meal, a piece of me thought for just a sliver of a moment that perhaps I might not belong here. I thought about what my friends back home told me the night before and how they laughed at me and especially how my two black friends, Kahlil and Joe, city dwellers themselves from Brooklyn and Atlanta, looked at me like I was a very stupid kid.

# Chapter 5

## Fences

When I finally walked over to the courts, still dribbling my ABA ball, I saw they were alive with basketball games. There was a bleacher next to the first court and there was an empty seat on the very top bleacher, so I climbed up and sat by myself and watched the games. There were black people in the bleachers, and they pretended to ignore me, but after a few minutes, I could see quick looks from old black men and young black women. They looked away when they saw that I saw that they were looking at me. I heard a few mumbled words I think were meant for me, but I tried to ignore them.

What I couldn't ignore was the game in front of me. It was magic. Ten young black men were engaged in a kind of basketball ballet I had never witnessed before. Their speed was remarkable as they raced up and down the court. Some of them were short and muscular, while others were tall and lean and sinewy. All of their bodies glistened with sweat in the gathering darkness. Their eyes were bright under the city lights that burned fully over the Cranston Street courts. They whipped bullet passes and dribbled between their legs and leaped impossibly high to snatch passes or swat shots into the night or dunk and hang on the metal rims of the basketball backboard. With every great pass or dribble or shot or dunk, the crowd that had gathered around the court, at least one hundred strong by then, would let out a "Whoop" or "Damn" or "That's what I'm talking about!" The players trash talked with each other or trashed talked with people in the stands or basically trash talked with anyone near the court. The trash talking was indiscriminate and it was fascinating, and I found myself not breathing as I watched one majestic dunk or rainbow jump shot or behind-the-back pass after another. The more I watched, the more the game pulsed in my blood and I felt myself drawn oddly and fatefully down to the court.

I picked up my old gym bag and my ABA basketball and stepped down the creaky, grey bleachers past two old black men with bald heads and huge bellies. I said, "Excuse me," and they looked up and saw my whiteness in the silhouette of the Providence night and they didn't move a single inch. I said, "Excuse me" again and stepped carefully around them so I wouldn't touch them. I jumped down off the last bleacher and landed as gracefully as I could, even though now I knew that every black man and black woman and black child in the bleachers or surrounding the court was watching me. This time their eyes did not look away when I looked at them.

I saw deep, ebony faces or dark chocolate complexions or creamy brown appearances. But what really drew me in was the luminescence of their eyes. They smoldered with sharpness and intensity and colors and emotions and intelligence and curiosity. Some eyes were deep and dark and matched their faces while others were incredibly blue like the colors of the sea during a storm. Their piercing eyes followed me as I walked the length of the chain link fence that surround the concrete world of the court. I stepped toward an opening in the fencing where other black men stood and once again, I said, "Excuse me."

The black men at the gate to the court had seen me sitting in the bleachers and they saw me walk towards them like every other black face at the court that night. They stepped aside. It was almost like they were slightly amused to see some white boy who thought he might actually get into the game. One of them grunted when I moved through the gate and another one chuckled and this young black woman put her hands on her hips and kind of shifted her weight to one side and looked at me like, "Who the hell is this?" I tried not to make eye contact, but it was impossible because her eyes held me like her eyes owned me. I couldn't look away until I finally passed her.

I walked over to the side of the court under the basket where other young black men waited to get in the game. I leaned against the part of the chained fence that separated one court from the other court where lesser players tried to impress enough to get into the big game. The chained fence was rusted and had pieces of iron that looked more like prison wire than chain-linked fencing. The iron had an orange hue that contrasted against the deepening black evening sky.

I put down my basketball and squatted down next to my gym bag. I pulled out my favorite ball-playing basketball t-shirt with the image of Pete Maravich that was just about worn off since I wore that shirt so many times playing in other pick-up basketball games. I took off my polo shirt and put the Pete Maravich shirt on as quickly as I could. I took my dirty running shoes and old sweat socks off and pulled out a pair of fuzzy grey socks I always wore when I played ball, however horribly they might stink. I wiggled my feet into the socks and adjusted them so they would ball up just above my ankles. Feeling my socks were perfect, just like they had to be every time I played, I reached into the bag once more and pulled out my perfectly white Converse All-Star high cut basketball shoes.

Before my dad and me left West Beaumont, I made sure to change out the laces. I had replaced creamy white laces with a set of blue laces and another set of gold laces. I had threaded both pairs of laces into my perfectly white All-Star hoop shoes so I could wear the colors of my hometown with pride. I knelt down and placed my right foot into my right-sided sneaker. I concentrated on making sure that the laces were not too tight and not too loose. I wanted my foot to be one with the sneaker. I double-knotted the laces when I tied them up and then deliberately put my left foot into the left-sided perfectly white hoop shoe and went through the same, exact ritual of pulling the blue and gold laces just tight enough, and then double-knotted them. I tied my shoes the same way whether I was putting on hoop shoes or football cleats or track spikes. I guess I was OCD about the whole thing, but everything on my feet from the shoes and socks and laces had to be perfect before I could play.

Finally, when my hoop shoes and laces and floppy socks were as perfect as I could make them, I looked up. The game had come to a complete stop and every black face on the court and in the stands stared at me. I mean, the game had stopped while I had laced up my hoop shoes. One player stood with incredibly long arms hanging down almost to his knees. He chewed gum while he stared at me. Another shorter player folded his arms over his barrel-chest. His face was set like black granite. A third player put his muscular arm on the shoulder of another player, this one with a tremendous afro and a red sweat band wrapped around his forehead just below his hair line. I tried to look tough, but I knew I was failing, so I just took my red, white, and blue ABA basketball and my gym bag and moved off to the corner of the court where I thought that perhaps I would become invisible if I just stood motionless.

The kid with the barrel chest spit on the cracked and broken concrete and the game resumed. For the moment, I did feel invisible, not because I wasn't there, but because the black people ignored me like I wasn't there. New players showed up and teams were made, and players called, "We got next," and I waited for I don't know what because it was clear I wasn't going to be getting in any game. What did I know about inner-city basketball and black kids who lived and breathed in the projects and run-down duplex apartments on Cranston Street? I waited to get in, but I was just ignored because the black players didn't care, or I was just ignored because the black players did care. I didn't know, but I stayed at the park for what seemed like hours. I wanted in their game.

Finally, one of the players on the same team as the guy with the huge afro and red head band said he had business he needed to take care of. He left the court with his team having won the last five games. They swore at him and the guy with the extremely long arms called him a pussy and the barrel-chested guy said, "Stay home next time, you fat crap." There were plenty of players available, but even I knew there was a pickup-game code. You don't switch from your team and join the champion's team. It's simply not done.  It wasn't done in West Beaumont, and evidently it was not going to happen here on the Cranston Street courts.  I stepped away from my invisibleness and tried to look cool and held my ABA ball under my right armpit.  The guy with the afro and red head band deliberately tried to look at anyone else on the court except me, but he was in a bind because he didn't want to leave the court, and if he couldn't find a fifth player, he would have to give up his precious right to play.

A little flutter tickled my gut.  Finally, he turned and faced me and without any air of enthusiasm, he changed my life and his life forever.

"White boy, you wanna run?"

# Chapter 6

## White Boy

I opened my old gym bag as wide as I could get it and stuffed my ABA Julius Irving basketball into the bag along with my other sneakers and my polo shirt. I pulled out a ragged towel I used to mop sweat off of me because, you know, I sweat a lot when I run. I took my gym bag that now looked like a pregnant pig and I set it down out of bounds near half court. I ran onto the court trying to look cool and like I belonged. The guy with the afro and red head band told me to go cover some guy who had long dreads and shorts that barely hung onto his hips. The guy had crooked teeth and a bit of a chin beard and stubby calf muscles and thick ankles. He wasn't very good, which I figured out pretty quick because no one passed him the ball. He ran around the court waving his hand in the air like, "I'm open, give me the damn ball," but not one pass came his way. So basically, I kind of followed him around and watched the game unfold.

The other players on his team were very good. They had been waiting on the sideline for maybe three games until it was their turn. One guy was about 6'7' and wore a "LaSalle" maroon and white basketball jersey. His shoulders stuck out like two jagged cliffs and his elbows were polished jackknifes. His name was Leon and he seemed to be in charge of his team. The guy on my team with the long arms that dangled down to his knees, he picked up Leon. Long Arms could jump, but LaSalle was wide, and his shoulders were mountains of muscle and Long Arms couldn't keep him away from the basket. LaSalle hit face up jumpers and he dropped his pivot foot and did this graceful fall-away jump shot and he was beautiful and graceful and supernatural to watch. Finally, he head-faked Long Arms. Long Arms jumped to block Leon's shot, but Leon deftly waited for Long Arms to reach the apex of his jump. Leon dribbled with his left hand and raced along the baseline and elevated to an incredible height.  He had the ball in his two hands and when he leaped, he rotated 360 degrees and tomahawked the ball with such force, the basketball pole that was cemented into the concrete of Cranston Street Park shook and shimmied like a California skyscraper about to crash during an earthquake.  Leon held onto the basket with the chain link netting and lifted both of his enormous feet level with his hands.  He let out a deep, guttural, "Ah!" and let go of the rim.  He fell back to our planet and immediately turned to face Long Arms.  He put his nose against Long Arm's nose and stared venomously like their private war was now won and Leon was the undisputed king of the court. The sidelines and the stands and anyone nearby who saw Leon's dunk let out, "Whoops" and everyone laughed at the dominance of Leon and the disgrace of Long Arms.  I jogged along the sideline of the court and kept my distance and tried once again to be invisible.  I didn't know whether to let out my own "Whoop," but something told me to just shut up and run down the court, so that's what I did.

The kid with the barrel chest took the ball up court for big afro red head band's team, of which I guess I was a token member.  Some kid about his height but nowhere near his muscularity tried to stay with Barrel Chest, but after dribbling between his legs with dizzying speed and then a quick jab with his left foot and a behind the back dribble, the guy covering Barrel Chest collapsed onto the cracked concrete.  They call that getting your ankles broke, which basically means that you suck and the guy with the ball owns you. Barrel Chest drove the lane, and just as Leon came over to swat his shot, Barrel Chest zipped a pass to the corner where big afro, red head band guy was waiting.  He collected the pass and in one graceful motion, ascended into the evening and seemed to hold his elevation longer than possible.  With the ball in his left hand and his right hand as a guide, big afro, red head band guy snapped his wrist and followed through with his finger-tips.  The ball spun perfectly and impossibly high into the night, almost disappearing into its blackness. After a moment of invisibility, the ball arced gracefully down from the heavens. It nestled into the chain link netting of the basket and made this metallic, crushed-can sound.

I found myself with my mouth wide open because I had never seen a jump shot done with such precision and grace and elevation. It didn't seem possible that a ball launched that high could find the net, but the crowd erupted again and more "Whoops" exploded from the onlookers. Big afro red head band guy pointed at Barrel Chest and ran back on defense. People on the sideline shouted out, "Marcus!" so being smart, I figured that was his name. Marcus high fived and low fived the people watching the game. He shouted out, "Nice look, Ray," so I figured that Ray was the kid with the barrel chest. Long Arms ran down the court and gave Marcus a quick tap on the butt to which Marcus quietly said, "Thanks, Henry," so now I at least knew the names of four of the guys on the court; Marcus, Ray, Leon, and Henry. They would later become names etched into my soul, but at that moment, they were just four guys who were black and who were very, very good at playing hoop.

The other team came down the court. The guy I was covering had long since tried to get open. He was cursing and muttering and complaining that he never got the ball, so one of the guys on the team shouted, "Here you go, then. Do something with it." The guy I was covering caught the ball and laughed and yelled out, "Watch out, white boy." He dribbled to his right with his right hand and went between his legs a couple times, but always came back to his right hand. Instead of being smart and letting him do his thing, I reached across with my left hand and flipped the basketball away and stole the ball and bolted. I found myself dribbling full speed down the left-hand side of the court. I heard a few "Whoops," but I think they were more intended for the guy I had just picked clean, like the crowd "Whooped" a mocking jeer. But what did I know?

I raced down the court, and by this time, Leon had reacted to my steal and chased after me. He was fast and he was enormous, and he had every intention of swatting my layup across the darkness of the Cranston Street Park. But I knew this was exactly what he wanted to do. Let's put the white boy in his place and show him he does not belong here. I remembered just a few nights ago when I made a steal and that older white kid tried to block my shot, so nature took over, and just as I was about to launch into my layup, I flipped the ball across the right side of my body and got crashed into, this time by an enormous black mountain. He drove me into the cracked pavement of the court and fell on top of me. I felt like I was being smothered by an avalanche, and I couldn't breathe, and I was sure I was being crushed. But my pass had caught Leon off guard. It settled into the large hands of big afro red head band Marcus.

He had chased after the play because he wanted to see my shot demolished, just like every black person who watched from the court or the sidelines or the rickety stands wanted to see. But the ball was in his hands now, and his instincts took over and he leaped high into the night and made a two-handed slam where he also hung from the rim and let out his own "Ah!" Now the whoops were real and the cheering loud and I could hear them even though I was being compressed under the mountainous mass that was Leon. He got up and yelled out, "Damn!" I didn't know if the "Damn" was meant for my pass or for Marcus' dunk, but he said it again and this time it was a loud "Damn!" And I knew it was because I made the pass and maybe even embarrassed him.

I picked myself up and made sure nothing was broken and ran back to get on defense. The guy I was covering just stood off to the side with his arms folded, with a look on his face like he knew something was coming. I left him alone and kind of settled into the three second area to help on defense. Someone passed the ball to Leon, and for some reason, Henry with the long arms just kind of stood out of the way instead of staying with Leon and playing defense. Marcus made this "ole" kind of motion and Leon took two quick dribbles and drove to the basket. I should have left well enough alone and let Leon dunk on me and reset the balance of the court and the galaxy, but what did I know?

I made two quick shuffle steps of my own and positioned myself in the direct line of Leon's dunk. He drove his knee high above his waist and took the ball in one hand like he was going to be so high in the air, he could just throw the basketball down into the chain-linked netting. But I was stupid. I let him crash into me, taking a charge like I always tried to do back in West Beaumont, but this wasn't West Beaumont. This was the Cranston Street Park and it was the heat of the summer in the blackest part of Providence, and you don't take charges on basketball courts like that. Leon crashed full force into me, and my body was driven backwards. I could see Leon's enormous form above me as he yelled out another, "Ah!" I slammed into the concrete and my head whiplashed backwards, cracking into the concrete. I saw the stars of the Providence night begin to dim and finally blacken out, and I swirled off into the edge of an obscure foreign universe.

# Chapter 7

## Walk You Home

When I started to come around and the nighttime stars began to come into focus, I sat up and reached up and felt a wet face cloth that someone must have put against my face when I was blacked out. I kind of shook my head like you do when you've smacked your skull against concrete. I let out a low groan and looked around and saw that the basketball court and the stands and the fenced area was devoid of people, except for this huge mountain of a black kid and this guy with astonishingly long arms and some kid with nothing but muscles and a barrel chest and this kid with an incredibly tall afro and a red head band. I looked at them for a few seconds. They seemed amused. They had smirks on their faces and kept their arms folded across their chests. The kid with the afro, who I now remembered to be Marcus, sat on the lowest bleacher and held my ABA red, white, and blue basketball between his legs and methodically dribbled it back and forth between his knees with just the slightest movement of his fingertips, like dribbling a basketball was something he was born doing.

"You awake, white boy?"

"I think so. Let me check."

I tried to stand up, but the night began to spin again, and the enormous mountain of a kid came over to me and put his hand out to help me from falling and embarrassing myself.

"Take your time. No hurry. I'm surprised you alive, the way your head smacked concrete."

I took his enormous hand and let him help me steady myself because at that point, I was pretty sure I wasn't going to be able to do it on my own.

"You stupid or something? You took a charge, on Leon? That

stupid or what, Henry?"

The kid with the muscles and the barrel chest whose name was Ray, laughed and looked over at Henry.

"He stupid," Henry laughed a little bit in this very high-pitched laugh that people make when they inhale helium. "Stupid."

"Maybe I was stupid," I tried to say as I got to my feet and let go of Leon's man hand and felt the world spin again and grabbed back on to keep from falling over.

Leon laughed at me again and said, "No hurry," and this time I tried to slow down how my body moved and how my eyes spun. I tried to talk slower.

"I never got run over by a mountain before," I said to Leon and looked up maybe half a foot because Leon was at least that much taller than me. "I guess maybe I was stupid."

"You stupid," Henry cackled this time and the rest of the guys laughed hard at me but there was nothing I could do but put on an idiotic grin that just made them laugh even harder. Ray with the barrel chest fell off the bleacher and rolled on the concrete and howled and pointed at me and laughed even harder.

"Taking a charge on Leon! You must be kidding me!"

They all seemed to be having a wonderful time at my expense, except for Marcus, the kid with the enormous afro and the bright red head band. He looked at me with serious eyes and no expression on his face like he was trying to figure out what the hell he was looking at. The rest of the guys stopped laughing after a while and they looked at Marcus and saw that he wasn't laughing so they calmed down a bit and waited for Marcus to speak.

"Where you from, white boy?"

# Chapter 8

## Defense

Marcus kept his cold, hard stare fixed on me. My eyes were just about clear, and I didn't feel like I was wobbling anymore as I bent over to wipe some of the dirt from the basketball court off my knees and stood up and slapped away the grit that was stuck to my backside. I looked at Marcus and his afro and then at Henry and Leon, and then at Ray and back to Marcus.

"I'm from across the street, the grey duplex over there," I pointed to my Meme and Poppy's house like I figured that my wise-ass answer would be enough of an explanation, which of course it wasn't. If I was a white kid living in their neighborhood they would have, in fact, known of my existence, so I decided perhaps I shouldn't be such a wise ass.

"I mean, that's my grandparents' house. I'm from Massachusetts; West Beaumont, Massachusetts." They looked at me like I was telling them about some undiscovered planet. "Just north of Boston."

"Nothing but white people north of Boston," Ray kind of laughed and the other guys laughed too except, again, for Marcus.

He kept his eyes fixed on me. I felt like a bug under a microscope or how some kids use magnifying glasses to burn insects or worms or other disgusting creatures that they think are unworthy of mere existence.

"I ain't never been to Boston."

Marcus spoke in this slow, even cadence, like my dad spoke because my dad used to be a Marine and that's how Marines taught my dad to speak. Marcus' words were slow and deliberate and carefully measured, like he thought out each word before he decided he was going to use it.

"I ain't never been outside of Providence. Never felt the need."

"Us neither," piped in Ray and Henry. "I mean, Leon been outside, playing basketball for LaSalle." Ray said the La in LaSalle like it was pronounced "Lay-Salle", which I thought was funny, so I laughed a little bit, but no one else laughed so I stopped.

"New York City, Baltimore, Hartford." Leon spoke with this low rumble like the sound boilers make in the bowels of a high school; always burning inside but never exploding. "Just city ball. No country, West Beaumont ball."

Leon made sure to say country with just the smallest emphasis, like the country was where I lived, and it was no place for him. Which wasn't true, because, you know, there were black people in the "country" of West Beaumont and our town let in like ten of them, and hell, I knew two; Kahlil and Joe, so I thought Leon was wrong.

I shifted my feet a bit and waited a second or two and then said stupidly, "You all should come to West Beaumont sometime." I said "you all" like I was trying to speak black. It was a mistake. Marcus eyes never left mine, even when I was trying to look at Leon and Ray and Henry. I was drawn back to looking at him. I didn't know him, at all, but I could sense a power to his gaze. It had strength and dignity and was completely not what I thought I would see in him.

"You trying to speak black?" Marcus took a step closer.

"I'm not trying to speak black."

"Maybe you should just stop talking."

"Ok. I'll stop talking," I kept talking.

These four black guys continued to look me up and down like I was some sort of life form they had yet to encounter.

"I'm curious. What made you think we going to let you run with us?"

Ray and Henry and Leon took a step closer to me. It was still stifling hot for this late at night. I felt the air sucked out around me and I had a difficult time pulling air back into my lungs.

"I thought I could just get in a game. I just wanted to play."

"Just like that. Run in our game, white boy?"

Marcus took a second step and now we were about five feet apart, and for the first time, and maybe I should have felt this already, but for the first time since the game started, I began to get nervous. I thought about what Michael and James said to me back in West Beaumont when I told them I was coming to Providence. I remembered talking to Kahlil about visiting him at Co-Op City in Brooklyn and how he said that maybe I shouldn't, and now, I began to understand.

"Hey, I don't want trouble. I just wanted in a game."

"What makes you think you in trouble?" Marcus asked, and for the first time, his facial expression changed from a cold, hard stare to one of being a little pissed off. He sucked in his cheeks and his eyebrows narrowed, and the skin on his forehead got all tight.

"You think all black people want to beat up crackers like you?"

"Maybe we should do what he think we gonna do: whip his ass." Ray took the basketball that he held in his hands and he bent over and began to bounce the ball hard and fast, but his eyes never left mine and this tiny smile formed on his lips. Henry laughed when Ray said what he said and so did Leon and now all four of them stepped closer, so they began to violate my personal space.

"You guys are violating my personal space," I said quickly.

The four of them just looked at me and then bust out laughing like this was the funniest thing they had ever heard.

"Violating yo personal space. Shit! That the most *white* thing I think I ever heard. Violate yo personal space!"

Ray fell down again like he did before and rolled on the concrete and started coughing because he was laughing so hard. When the four of them stopped laughing, Leon stepped closer and put his enormous meat hook of a hand on my shoulder.

"I like this white boy. He stupid, that fo sure, but I like him. Personal space! Haw!"

"Breathe, white boy. You ain't dying tonight. What's your name?" Marcus smiled for the first time.

"Tim."

"Well, Tim, you got some rocks for playing with us. I'll give you that. But we here are the nice black guys in Providence."

With that, the smallest amount of oxygen began to transfer in and out of my alveoli and the muscles at the back of my neck began to relax just a bit.

"But how you think you gonna make it back across the park to yo Meme and Poppy's house? They be some black folk who ain't as nice as we be."

Marcus' smile widened, but it seemed to me that his smile wasn't that things are funny kind of smile but the like, you might actually die tonight smile. I looked across the park back toward my Meme and Poppy's house and the night was black except for one remaining street light that had not been broken. I squinted, and I could make out a few groups of faceless men and women sitting on the park benches or walking along the sidewalk or standing in the shadows on the street corner. A car in the distance gunned its engine and far away a police car screamed, and a gunshot rang out not far away, over by the bocce courts where the French-Canadian men played when there were still enough of them around.

"I'll get home."

I tried to say it confidently like a stupid sixteen-year-old who thinks he knows everything and is immortal might try to sound. It came out hollow and Marcus kind of laughed.

"He stupid," Henry laughed again. Ray and Leon did too but not like the way they laughed at me before.

"He is ill-advised. Maybe we should walk this white boy back to his Meme and Poppy's house." Marcus looked at his friends. "What you think, fellas?"

"He let me bowl him over. Knocked himself out. Lived to tell the tale. Let's keep him from dying, at least for tonight."

Leon nodded toward my Meme and Poppy's house. The others started to move in that direction, so I grabbed my gym bag and my red, white, and blue ABA Julius Irving basketball and walked behind these four black kids who evidently would rather I didn't die that night.

Suddenly, I stopped at the edge of the concrete court and said, "Wait," and knelt down and took off my perfectly white, Converse All-Star basketball shoes. I carefully untied my shoes and pulled out my sweaty feet and rolled off the old, fuzzy grey socks. I put on my walking-around sneakers and stuffed the grey socks into my gym bag. When I went to carefully place my perfectly white All-Stars into the gym bag, I could see dark smudges along the toe and sides of the shoes. I said, "Damn" and took out one of the fuzzy grey socks from the bag. I used it like a wash cloth and tried to wipe off the smudges. The more I tried, the darker they became. Marcus and Leon and Ray and Henry started to laugh a bit but stopped when they saw how furiously I was trying to clean my shoes back to their perfection. After a minute, I defeatedly bent my head down and began to put the basketball shoes in my gym bag. My white Converse All-Star basketball shoes were no longer perfectly white, and I knew they were darkened forever just because I thought it would be fun to play basketball in the heat of Providence.

# Chapter 9

## Pele

When I thought I was finally over having my white basketball shoes smudged, I grabbed my gym bag and walked off the court. Leon rumbled along like a large truck. Ray kind of darted forward, something like a water bug might dart on the water when it's trying to avoid prey. Henry didn't so much walk as he loped along, taking one stride for every two of Ray's. Marcus kind of glided, almost like he and the broken pavement and kicked-up dust of the park were fully a part of his essence. He slowed down his floating motion and waited for me to catch up. His feet seemed to be at once fully part of the concrete and also hovering at the same time. He was about my height and weight, with a thin waist and impossibly skinny ankles. I was a track guy and I guess it's weird, but I always looked at the ankles of people to see if they could run or not. My dad told me once that people with skinny ankles make great runners. Marcus had the skinniest ankles I had ever seen, which explained why he could jump so high and run so fast on the court.

The other thing I noticed was that Marcus wore high top basketball shoes just like me. What wasn't like me was his basketball shoes were old and beaten and ripped at the toes. The laces looked like they had snapped countless times. There were knots that ran from the toes up the length of the sneaker until finally to where the bow was barely fastened. I could see the laces straining against his foot and shoe like they might break at the slightest movement. I thought of my double laced, blue and gold brand-new shoe strings. There was no need to replace them before I came to Providence. But I did, probably because I could.

Marcus noticed me noticing his sneakers. We made eye contact and I thought about his sneakers compared to mine. I was aware deep inside that my sneakers were better than his and that my sneakers were sneakers that I had to protect. I zipped up my gym bag self-consciously so my precious hoop shoes would be kept safe. Marcus just stared at me. He didn't say anything. He was a statue standing resolute on a battlefield not of his choosing, but a battlefield nonetheless. I started to think that my conflict was simply getting back to my Meme and Poppy's house. I appreciated Marcus walking me back, but I didn't grasp what that would mean for Marcus. How could I? I looked at him and then I looked around the park and saw groups of dark people in the shadows of Cranston Street. They were talking or smoking or drinking impossibly large beer bottles. It was not my world. I guess I was glad of that, nervous as I was.

Leon and Henry and Ray waved as they disappeared down one end of Cranston Street. Marcus turned away from them and down to the other side of Cranston Street. There was a group of black men drinking on the corner. Two women walked quickly past them. They must have said something to the women because the women stopped abruptly and turned back. They took two very quick steps forward and I could see that whatever the men just said, these two women were not going to let it pass. The confrontation took only seconds, but even though I didn't live here, I felt the electricity of the confrontation. It seemed to grow very quiet on Cranston Street. Whatever was going on between the two women and the men, Marcus was acutely aware. I could see his chest move slowly, up and down. His breathing made a deep roll that I could hear from where I was standing ten feet away. It sounded like the churning of a great engine straining to life after sitting dormant for too long.

Without looking, Marcus said, "Come on, white boy." I moved quickly with him as we crossed Cranston Street to the same side where the men stood about fifty feet away. The two women said what they needed to say. It silenced the men on the corner, at least for a few seconds. As the two women walked off, one of the men shouted out, "Bitch" and the rest of the men laughed and drank some more from their enormous beer bottles. The two women quickened their pace. Their long strides brought them quickly to near where we were standing. They had to pass in front of Beauchamp's house before they reached Marcus, who seemed to be waiting for them. Even though it was late at night, Beauchamp sat on his rocker, just like he was doing when I left my Meme and Poppy's house hours earlier when it was blazing hot and the sun had yet to set. Now it was just hot, like deep in the summer nighttime hot. Beauchamp had changed out of his wife-beater t-shirt. I could see new tobacco stains on what used to be a white polo. Years of tobacco stains had turned it into something resembling the color of a sick, yellow pee from an old cat. We were downwind of Beauchamp. I could smell his body odor and the tobacco juice from where I stood next to Marcus. When the two women approached us, Beauchamp let fly another stream of sickly green juice. But his aim was off, and the juice flew behind the two women. I heard him say, "Shit" and he leaned back on his rocker and put one foot up on the railing of his porch. I wondered if he ever slept.

The two women spied me standing next to Marcus. If it surprised them or bothered them, it didn't show. They walked directly to Marcus. It was at that point that I had my first good look at them. They were stunning. The taller of the two extended two slender and fit arms and wrapped them around Marcus neck. She kissed him on the cheek and looked to be his mirror image. She had a strong afro that seemed to glow from the single street light that shined down and illuminated where she stood, like a spotlight shines on a single dancer. She had high cheekbones like I imaged an African princess would have. Her eyes sparkled from the beam of the street light and they danced with intelligence. Her neck was long and elegant as it disappeared down into her rose-colored blouse. A thin exposure of waist showed from wear the blouse ended and her blue jeans began. Her hips widened out gracefully toward her extraordinarily long legs. Her ankles were thin, just like Marcus', and she wore silver sneakers that highlighted the ebony of her ankles. I caught myself staring and quickly moved my eyes up to meet hers. I was a captive of her eyes, so beautiful were they, yet so challenging of me. They held me with curiosity and a bit of whimsy, like "What is a white boy doing in Providence on Cranston Street after sunset?" She clearly was Marcus' sister, so completely did she mirror his form and expression.

"Who's the white boy?" she kind of laughed as her eyes held me prisoner. "Is he with you, Marcus, and if so, why is that, may I ask?"

Her diction was perfect, and I was taken aback by it.

"This is Tim. He ran with us tonight. Thought I'd walk him home, being as late as it is. White boy, this is my sister, Sherri."

"What, may I ask, are you doing in my neighborhood?"

"He staying with Armand and Concorde. The French-Canadians in this duplex."

Marcus pointed to where my Meme and Poppy lived, and Sherri nodded her head once.

"I know your grandparents. They're quiet and keep to themselves, but they're good people. They always say hello when Evelyn and I walk by."

She said it loud enough for Beauchamp to hear. He was still rocking in his chair, eavesdropping on everything being said. He leaned to his side and let out another quick spit of tobacco juice. It splattered next to one of his work shoes that he still wore on his feet. It added to the puddle of juice that grew from a night of spitting. Sherri looked at her friend. She was shorter and more compact.

"This is Evelyn," Marcus said as his eyes angled down to Evelyn's eyes.

Her hair was cut tight to her scalp. Her neck was solid; not masculine solid, but athletically solid. She wore a black and gold pendant that hung around her neck. Her yellow blouse had a plunging neckline that revealed strong, full breasts. Her blouse was tucked into yellow pants that came well up above her waist. The pants were fastened with three buttons found on the side of her waist. The pants covered strong, short thighs. They ended in tapered bell-bottoms that covered high heels that hid the fact that she was much shorter than Sherri. She looked quickly at me and then back over her shoulder to where the group of men were still drinking beers. Her eyes darted back and forth between me and the beer drinkers. She seemed scared, but I kept my mouth shut because by this point, I had figured out that maybe I should just keep quiet since I was almost inside my Meme and Poppy's house and I just might survive the night.

Maybe that was wishful thinking, because right at that moment, the group of beer-drinking men started striding toward where the four of us stood. I had been nervous up to that point, being I was probably the only white kid within two miles. But when they got closer, I felt my throat begin to squeeze and my trachea thicken, and it was becoming very difficult to breathe. The tiny hairs on the back of my neck stood up, and I found myself clutching my ABA basketball to my chest with one hand and tightening the grip on my gym bag with my precious Converse All-Stars hiding at the bottom with the other. Marcus stepped forward and placed his body in front of me as the men converged. There were five of them. They were expressionless. I could sense both Sherri and Evelyn tense fully and I saw their enormous eyes widen. I don't think they thought the men would follow them, but here they were, and clearly, Sherri and Evelyn were frightened.

"Marcus."

The leader of the group stepped out from the rest of the men.

"Pele."

Marcus held his ground as Pele took another step forward. If Marcus was scared, it didn't show. He dropped his chin slightly and raised his eyes so it looked like Marcus was trying to see under Pele's gaze, like considering the soul of the man. Pele's eyes had no depth. The darkness of his pupils seemed fathomless, like the depths of some vast ocean devoid of life. He was skinny, with long black pants that drew down to polished, pointy black boots. His hands were thin and long. He wore an expensive watch on his left wrist. His arms were willowy. Not skinny, but taut, like a snake's body coiled in hiding. His mouth was pencil thin and there were no creases from smiling. He stared back at Marcus until finally, he lifted his forehead up and shifted his gaze toward me. I was frozen in place, not the way Sherri had me frozen in awe. I was frozen in terror. Pele looked down at the Cranston Street sidewalk and he spat once. The spittle bounced off the ground.

"What you doin' here?"

"He ran with us tonight. Walking him home, Pele. He live with Armand and Concorde."

"Whites. French-Canadian Whites." Pele said it and spat again. It was another powerful spit. He added no more emotion to his spit than a stray cat would have devouring a street rat.

His eyes held me, and I felt tiny. I finally forced myself to look away when I heard the door to Beauchamp's house close quickly. His chair continued to rock until it was almost motionless. The light in Beauchamp's window went dark and the shade was pulled down.

"He with you, so I let the cracker be, for the time being." He turned his eyes back to Marcus and then moved them up and down the length of Sherri and Evelyn. "You look fine tonight. Why you leave us hanging back there? We just being polite." He hissed it more than he said it.

Once again, I could see the muscles in Marcus neck flex while Sherri and Evelyn tried to look brave in front of Pele. I would have thought they were being brave until Pele made the slightest motion toward Sherri and Evelyn. He couldn't have moved more than an inch or two, but it was enough that Marcus stepped quickly in front of his sister and Evelyn. Pele's four buddies remained motionless behind him, maybe about four or five steps, lurking where the lone street lamp did not cast enough light for me to see their faces. They scared me too, but not as much as Pele.

"Just heading home, Pele. It's late and Sherri and Evelyn have work in the morning. Tim, why don't you move along back to your grandparent's house? You ran well tonight. Maybe we let you run with us again."

He didn't say, "You ran well for a white boy." He just said I ran well, and stupidly, that was more important to me at that moment than the fear I had of being in the presence of obsidian evil. I moved behind Marcus and Sherri and Evelyn, and still clutching my gym bag and basketball to my chest, I jogged across Cranston Street, over to my Meme and Poppy's duplex. There was still a light on in the living room and as I hopped up the stairs to the front door, faster than perhaps I wanted anyone to notice, I could see the little TV in the living room still on and the form of my Poppy leaning back in his chair. As I turned the knob to the front door, I looked back to see that Marcus and Pele were almost nose to nose. Sherri and Evelyn had taken a step back, but Marcus and Pele's voices were raised, and I could still hear what they were saying.

"It don't matter if you play ball. You play in my park. That mean you belong to me. You Cranston Street for life."

"I ain't part of yo gang, Pele. You let my sister and Evelyn be. We ain't got nothing to do with you and your horse and your coke. And stay away from Ray and Henry and Leon. They got their own lives. Let them be."

"I say who I let be on Cranston. Not you, Marcus. Your sister and Evelyn going to run product for me. Ain't that right Sherri? Ain't that right, Evelyn?"

Evelyn took a step closer to Marcus, so he was directly between her and Pele. Sherri stepped around her brother. She seemed to grow taller as she took a step toward Pele. Pele's buddies stepped closer, in unison. If I was a dog, the hair on the back of my neck would have stood straight up. I heard Poppy get up from his chair and turn off the TV. The darkness grew deeper.

"I ain't running for you, Pele. Not Evelyn either."

"You my woman once."

"I'm no one's woman."

I could see Sherri's face gently lit by the remaining light from the lamp post. It showed no emotion, but that stoic face was set in contrast to her eyes of fire. They danced and they mesmerized me, even from where I stood, and I couldn't see how Pele couldn't be undone by her. It was none of my business and had I known better, I would have gone inside my Meme and Poppy's house already, but since I hadn't, what I thought I saw was a woman owned by no one but herself. It made Pele look bad in front of his buddies.

"We'll see. Maybe not tonight. But you my woman and so is Evelyn. You best do what you know I want. You run for me. You sell my product. I can't have it no other way."

No one moved in the dark. Everyone held their own space in the universe. Something had to break.

"Move along, Pele. You heard my sister."

"Don't make me look bad in front of my boys. It won't stand."

"Move along, Pele. You got your answer."

"For now. Cranston mine, and everything on it."

Pele pivoted quickly and walked through his four buddies. They looked hard at Marcus and Sheri and Evelyn and then they spun around and shadowed Pele. What was left was a vacuum of air sucked up from Cranston Street that I could feel all the way up onto my Meme and Poppy's porch. I stepped into the darkened doorway and backed away, but I continued to peer out into the darkness. Marcus turned around in the opposite direction of Pele and followed his sister and Evelyn who had already scurried away. What I had just observed wasn't my world, but I still felt that some rule had been broken and the universe was out of balance. I knew enough about my world to know that when things got out of whack, balance had to reestablish. Maintaining balance in my world was not easy for a middle class, sixteen-year-old white kid and everything I thought were my world's big problems. I sensed that righting the balance of this world would be hard; hard like cracked concrete or hard like the snap of a bullet, the part of the night where there is fear and threat, and it scared me.

# Chapter 10

## My Meme

When I slipped in to my Meme and Poppy's duplex, I struggled to leave the night behind. Too many things had occurred in one night, and in the aftermath of the threat made towards Sherri and Evelyn, and how I witnessed it transpire, I was straining to understand it all, and I had just wanted to play basketball.

The living room was much darker than it was outside. The TV was off, and my grandfather was no longer in his recliner. I tried to be very quiet as I moved though the tiny living room and past the couch that stood next to the door of the bedroom that I would sleep in for the rest of the week. I nearly jumped out of my shoes when a dark form moved on the couch. It was my Meme. I could faintly make out her gold work shoes she wore when she hemmed the dresses and coats of the Italian families she worked for on the north side of Providence. She had thick ankles like some grandmothers have. There I go again looking at people's ankles. She lifted herself into a sitting position on the couch and reached over to turn on one of the ancient lamps my grandparents owned.

The light was very dim from the almost worn-out light bulb, but I could see her face clearly now as my eyes adjusted. She was old; maybe seventy. She had a pale, wrinkled face that hung down from her forehead. Her long dress had a brown and gold floral pattern that matched her work shoes. Her hair was curly and almost completely white. She wore cat-style glasses; the ones that have pointy edges. They lay on her chest, held to the back of her neck with a black shoe lace. I remember her telling me that she lost her glasses twice a day, even with the shoe lace. So I thought that was funny.

"Timothy, sit down next to me. You seem upset."

I sat next to her on the old couch. It was threadbare and thin so I could almost feel the springs through the cushions. My grandfather had spent years napping on this couch while listening to the Red Sox on the French-Canadian station out of Fall River. Sometimes, I wondered where the couch ended and my grandfather began.

I waited a few seconds before I looked at her. There were wrinkles that surrounded her eyes, but hers were not old-people's eyes. They twinkled with a kind of magic, like she knew things others didn't know and saw things in ways other people couldn't see. She was a quiet woman. She had raised my mother and her three brothers and took care of my grandfather while working sixty hours a week making sure the Italian families in North Providence looked stylish. She reached over and took my hand. They were like fish bones from years of sewing and hemming. But they were warm hands and they matched the warmth of her eyes and deepness of her smile.

"You come home late," she whispered in her heavy, French-Canadian accent.

She kept her voice low because my Poppy was asleep now and she knew he needed to get up early to go work as a tool maker at the factory across from the Cranston Street Armory.

"Were you worried about me, Meme?"

"Not until this moment."

"You weren't worried about me before while I was playing ball in the park?"

"No, of course not."

"Why wouldn't you be worried? This is Providence."

"Should I worry?"

"You're almost the only white family left here."

"This is true."

"And you aren't worried about that, Meme?"

I looked into her eyes. Mine shined with fear. Hers looked

curiously calm. I couldn't understand why she seemed so serene as I looked into her dark, chestnut eyes. I had just spent the better part of the night playing ball, getting knocked unconscious, and witnessing a dark thing between Marcus, his sister, and Pele. Surely, she had to understand what was happening around her duplex.

"Meme, why haven't you moved?"

"Why should I move? This is my home."

"Everyone else has gone, Meme."

"There are plenty of people here."

"I mean, all the white people."

It sounded odd coming out.

"They go. We stay. Your Poppy and me. This is our home."

I didn't understand what she was saying. Didn't she feel the fear that permeated Cranston Street? It was palpable to me. I could still feel the hatred between Marcus and Pele. Why didn't she?

"I work long days. I come home at night. I see other families. They work. They do the same. That's what I see. That's what they see, when they see me."

"Do you know Marcus? He has a sister, Sherri."

"I don't know Marcus well. I know Sherri. She's kind to everyone. She's kind to me, even when Beauchamp rocks on his porch, spitting his juice. She strides by him and ignores him. She ignores him because he is Beauchamp, not because he's white."

She took a deep breath and I could see her eyes begin to dance as she told me about Sherri.

"She helps me carry groceries. She helps me put them up in my cabinets because I don't reach so high anymore. She does it without me asking. She just does it because I am Concorde. Nice is nice, even in Providence."

"But what if Sherri wasn't here? She isn't the only black person on Cranston Street. There are some who are not so, I don't know, hospitable."

Meme cocked her head to one side like she was surprised by what I just said or at least what I said annoyed her. Now her eyes showed a blaze instead of a twinkle.

"I know what you say. You want me to move because I am white. Many people say so. I don't hear them. Not when they talk like the way you just spoke to me."

The blaze was now a fire. It startled me. Her eyes brushed me back and I squirmed away from her, just enough that she could see that her blazing eyes had their intended affect.

"You're a good boy. You play basketball tonight, *oui*? What did you see?"

I was silent for a moment. A lone car drove quickly past Meme's house.

"I saw that the black people at the court stared at me and I felt alone."

"They don't know you."

"I don't know them."

"No, you don't."

"And they know you, Meme?"

"Yes."

"And they don't see you're white?"

"No, they do see that I'm white. This is my world. I work. Your Poppy works. We are part of their world and they are part of ours. They are black and I see them. But I am white, and they see that too. They don't hate me because I should have left. They don't hate me because I stayed."

"So, you think if I lived here with you, I would be part of your

49

world and part of theirs?"

"No."

"Why not?"

"You're not black."

"Jesus, Meme, neither are you!"

Now I was getting mad and my eyes were probably smoldering. If they were, it didn't brush my Meme back. She sat solid and true on her couch in her duplex on Cranston Street and her eyes never strayed from me.

"You don't know them."

"I have black friends at home."

To this my Meme said nothing, like whatever I thought I knew about the world was so far off, so completely obtuse in my limited understanding, it didn't merit a response.

I looked at my Meme sitting in the faint light of her living room, and I realized I didn't understand her. Yeah, nice is nice. But this is Providence, and I hadn't seen much nice. What I saw scared me. I thought it should have scared my Meme.

"I still think you should move. You're almost all alone here."

"I hope you understand some day, Timothy. I don't think you staying with us for a few days will bring you understanding. Some people get stuck in a place and they can't get out."

Her eyes changed from blazing to weary, like years of understanding had sapped her strength.

"So why don't they move to a better place?"

"There are some rules that were made that helped some Americans and some rules that hurt. Most people here would move. They don't have the money to do it."

"They should just save up. Work, get a job, save up, and move out. Go someplace better than this."

I said it kind of derisively. My Meme noticed that too.

"So, that's all it takes?"

"I think so." It came out odd, like so many things I had said that night. "I just don't understand."

"Perhaps someday you will." She looked at me with those disarming, gentle eyes. I was too young to see her wisdom. She patted me on the leg. "Now your Meme is too tired to stay awake. Your Poppy might be lonely. I'm going to bed now. Your bed is made for you in the front bedroom. Sweet dreams."

It was late and I didn't think I could change her mind. Not that I really want to, but it just seemed like we were beyond each other's comprehension and it was time for bed, and I had enough of everything. I leaned over and looked her in the eyes.

"I love you, my Meme."

"Don't worry about me or your Poppy. This is home. We will die in this place."

I kissed her on her forehead. She pulled me even closer and wrapped her arms around me, so I was pulled close to her chest. I could feel her surprisingly strong heart beat almost in time with the sounds I could still hear outside. We sat there for a while. Perhaps Meme was trying to pass her understanding to me through her hug. Eventually, she let go and tried to get up. I helped her get off the couch. She adjusted her weight on first one foot then the other, letting her knees absorb her weight. She limped away from the living room with her gold shoes and her matching floral dress. She opened her bedroom door and stepped inside, but not before turning and giving just a hint of a smile and another sparkle of her eye. She blew me a kiss and closed the door to her bedroom where she and my Poppy slept since they moved to Cranston Street more than fifty years earlier.

I shut off the tiny light and turned around to make sure I knew the direction to my bedroom. I fumbled my way across the living room to the tiny bedroom I was to occupy for the next five nights.

The lone window to the bedroom was closed when I went in. I opened it up immediately and slightly less hot air swirled in from outside. I put down my ABA basketball and my gym bag with my high-top Converse All-Stars. I took my clothes out of my suitcase that my Meme had put in the tiny front bedroom for me. I opened up some drawers. The smell of moth balls burst forth and filled the room but was quickly overwhelmed by the smell of hot concrete and cigarettes and grills that had been warm not too long ago but now were burnt out. A faint stench of urine wafted in and I felt a gag reflex, but I was able to hold off. I really had nothing in my stomach to throw up anyway since I hadn't eaten anything since the fish I ate with my Meme and Poppy hours ago. I felt a deep hunger, but I was too tired to tiptoe back through the living room to the kitchen, so I took off my gym shorts and put on fresh underwear and lay down bare chested on the thin, flat mattress. The noises of the city continued, even though my portable alarm clock with the uranium glow showed 2:00 in the morning.

I found that even though I was starving and exhausted to my bones, I couldn't fall asleep. Too many things jostled in my brain. The more I tried to understand what had happened to me tonight, the more confused my thinking became. I thought about the faces of the black people at the basketball court as they stared at me like an alien from a different galaxy. I remembered waiting for hours until I finally got into the game, and then only because one of the guys on Marcus' team had to "take care of business," whatever that meant. I thought about massive Leon with the Lay Salle t-shirt straining against his impossible musculature. I thought about the incredible length of Henry's arms and how they almost hung down below his knees, and about the jack-rabbit quickness of Ray and his barrel chest, and I thought about Marcus knocking down jump shots from ridiculous orbits. Those guys didn't have to wait around for me when I got knocked out. Certainly, no one else seemed bothered by me being knocked unconscious. I don't know why they hung around until I came to, but after seeing Pele and the evil of his monotone voice and the depth of his lifeless eyes, I was glad they walked me home. Jesus, he scared me.

I thought about my Meme and Poppy and didn't understand how they could possibly remain on Cranston Street. There had to be a better place for them. And I also wondered about Beauchamp and why he hadn't moved out either. He was the only other white person within three miles, and even though he was white, I already hated him. As I lay there, in my single bed right next to the window, I thought about the notion of me hating Beauchamp, even though he was white. What did I mean by "even though?" Was I supposed to give him some slack for sticking it out when all the other white families had fled Cranston Street and much of Providence to move to towns like Rumford or South Kingston or across the state lines to Attleboro and Taunton? Were these places better for my Meme and Poppy and Beauchamp because these towns were mostly white? Sweat formed on my bare chest. I felt the deep heat that had been coursing around Cranston Street and New England that summer. It paralyzed me as I lay almost naked on my bed.

The answers seemed so obvious to me, but evidently, not so for my grandparents. I already felt like this week was going to be very long. I had witnessed the majesty of inner-city basketball and the dread of knowing that violence and fear roamed outside my window and would be there when I woke up. I started to close my eyes and understood the reality that I didn't need to stay here for long. Going back to West Beaumont was only five days away. I slept fitfully and dreamed of vast, belching smokestacks that engulfed the city with burning soot. It floated peacefully down and turned the people into ashen figures, trudging daily from one wasted destination to another.

# Chapter 11

## Hot Tar

I awoke the next morning, fully drenched in sweat, my boxers sagging off my hips as I opened the door and entered my Meme and Poppy's living room. I could smell sausage and eggs as I stumbled toward the kitchen, managing, of course, to stub my big toe on a chair leg. I stub a toe each day I live. I think if you look up the phrase, "stubbed toe" in the dictionary, you'll see my picture. I can't get out of my own way.

Scrambled eggs and sausage sat on the ancient, linoleum kitchen table. A glass of warm milk sat next to the now cooled breakfast plate. A note sat on the table where I could not possibly miss it. "Chores: Cut the grass, scrape the paint off the front porch, vacuum the living room, make your bed, wash the windows." Jesus. I came to Providence to relax and just spend time with me. Now Meme and Poppy had me as their personal honey-do. I smiled just a bit as I dug into my eggs. They were cold, but there was a hint of cheese, and that made them taste wonderfully. I realized how famished I was from not eating for almost 18 hours (it was now 10 AM).

My grandparents were long off to work. I took a sip of the milk, which like I said, was warm, and stretched my arms high above my head. I winced as my back and leg muscles flexed. I also felt a knob on the back of my head and remembered getting slammed into the concrete when Leon ran me over at last night's game. The knot swelled out about a half inch from my thick skull. I figured the injury wasn't fatal, so I dove back into the eggs and devoured the sausage without chewing much and leaned back in my chair and looked around my grandparents' kitchen.

It was old and it was dated, and it was spotless. The counter tops shined and the glass to the cupboards were clear. The kitchen floor was old linoleum that still had a sheen to it. The spaces under the cabinets had been vacuumed and not a piece of dust or food particle or dust bunny was anywhere to be found. I got out of my chair and went over to the stone sink and turned on the water and washed off my plate. I kept my hands under the stream of water and thought about the chores I had to do and the pick-up basketball games I wanted to play that night with Marcus and Leon and Henry and Ray. I blotted out the idea that Pele was out there somewhere and the threatening way he treated Sherri and Evelyn. I just wanted to play ball.

At that moment, pain shot through my hands. I had let the hot water continue to cascade from the faucet and stupidly, got my hands scalded. I screamed out and let slip the porcelain plate I had held moments before. It crashed into the stone sink and shattered. Shards of porcelain ricocheted within the deep sink. My hands were red from the scalding water. I quickly turned off the hot water and blasted my hands with cold water. The muscles in my body were fully tensed as I tried to hold my burned hands under the cold stream. After a few minutes, the cold water did its thing and the pain began to subside. I knew my Meme and Poppy didn't have much. The plate I just broke was one of six they owned. I would pay them back with the money I earned caddying at the country club in West Beaumont where I carried golf bags for rich doctors and lawyers and captains of industry.

I picked the porcelain shards out of the sink and carried them over to the trash can by the back door. I walked back to the kitchen table and looked at the list my Meme and Poppy left for me to do. Cutting the grass seemed easiest. I went back into my bedroom and grabbed some old shorts and a threadbare t-shirt and my every day sneakers. I walked out the back door and down the tiny steps to my grandparents' backyard. It was about a quarter of the size of the basketball court I played on the night before. There was a large grey fence surrounding it. Inside the fence on one corner of the yard, there was a trellis where strong and firm grape vines climbed. At the other corner was an old shed. It might have been red at one point in its existence, but now the color could only be guessed. Closer to faded rose, perhaps. The rest of the backyard was thick grass that clearly hadn't been mowed in a while. I opened up the shed and walked inside.

There was a long string hanging from the dark of the top of the shed. I pulled on it and a reluctant light popped on. The shed was filled with properly stacked yard tools: shovels and spades and hoes and grass clippers and hedge trimmers and hammers and cans of nails. There were bales of twine and spools of wire and work gloves and plastic eye protection. Sitting by itself on the shed floor was a relic of a mower. There was no engine to this tool. It was one of those mowers that cut grass when you pushed it and the power of your thrust turned the blade to cut the grass. I thought cutting the grass would be the easiest job on the list, especially because of the tiny square footage of the backyard. Still, I knew it was going to be a pain in the ass. But since my grandparents were going to feed me for a week, I knew I probably should cut the grass. I reached up and pulled down some grass-stained work gloves, put them on, and hauled the hand mower outside.

The sun was directly above me and its rays bore through me. The sky was a pallid blue from the polluted haze of the sky. And it was freaking hot. I hadn't done any work yet and my t-shirt had sweat stains leaking under my armpits and across my chest and down the small of my back. I turned the lawnmower to face the grass and pushed forward. The thick grass stopped the blades from turning. I pulled the push mower back to get some momentum and then drove it forward. The blades rotated somewhat, and some grass flew out from behind. I might have cut seven or eight inches and that was it. I pulled the mower back even farther and ran forward, driving my legs and pushing the mower in front of me with my straining arms. This time I managed to cut about two feet of grass. Good. Progress. I pulled the mower back again, intent on driving the old rig forward to the end of the patch of grass I was determined to cut, maybe about fifteen feet away. Racing as fast as I could, I lunged forward and drove the mower all the way to the end of the backyard. My legs burned and my chest heaved, and I stood up, happy with my success. I turned around and looked back. I had cut a strip of grass about twelve inches wide.

My t-shirt was fully enveloped in sweat and my calves were covered in blades of grass. I ran forward and drove the mower again and again until I could hardly breathe in the sweltering heat. I pulled myself up and put my hands behind my back and stretched by arcing my body so I looked into the sky. When I straightened back out, I heard a laugh. I looked down the alley between my grandparents' and Beauchamp's duplex. A black woman leaned against the gate of the alley. Her laugh kind of pissed me off. I dropped the handle of the push mower and walked toward her through the thin alley. I had it in my mind to tell her to go to hell because I was working and she had time to laugh, but when I got closer, I recognized her face. It was Sherri, Marcus' sister from the night before.

Even though I was pissed, seeing her translucent eyes completely disarmed me. I stopped short. Just like the night before, I could see that she was beautiful. Her hair was pulled back tight. Her neck was long and elegant and traveled beautifully down to a peach-colored, flowered blouse. I could see that her waist was trim beneath her blouse. She wore a thin, azure-blue skirt that was about knee length. Her dark legs tapered down to very skinny ankles and ended at white, short heels, each with a tiny bow on the toe. I don't know how long I was admiring her ankles, but it must have been too long.

"I'm up here."

Sherri said it with a bit of mischievousness, like I wasn't the only person who had admired her ankles before.

I looked up and she had a grin on her face. She put her hand up to her mouth and burst out a laugh. My white face turned crimson with embarrassment. I took off my work gloves that were now as soaked as my t-shirt.

"How long you been cutting Concorde's grass, white boy?" She took her hand off her mouth and put it on her right hip and kind of shifted her weight to one side. The grin on her face remained. I found myself lost in her eyes again, and even though I wasn't pushing the lawn mower, I began to sweat even more. She held a water bottle in her other hand. She laughed again and stuck her arm forward to offer me a drink. I hesitated a bit. I don't know why. She was being kind and offering water from her bottle.

"Go on, white boy. Drinking from my bottle won't kill you."

I think she guessed why I hesitated. Her smile disappeared. She had made the gesture in kindness and I didn't accept it immediately and I think she was pissed about it. I took a few steps forward and reached out my hand and took the bottle. I unscrewed the cap and looked at the rim for a minute to make sure there was nothing wrong with it before I drank two or three quick gulps. When I was done, I looked at the bottle again and then quickly wiped some water from my mouth and handed it back to her.

"Now is the time when you say thank you, or don't they teach manners from where you from?"

I looked at her for a few more seconds until the words, "Thank you" spilled out.

"Well, you're welcome," she said, and now the mischievous smile reemerged, like she couldn't keep it hidden for very long.

"You're that white boy from last night."

"Tim."

"Tim. That's right. You ran with Marcus last night. He told me about you."

"Don't you remember he introduced us last night?"

She thought about it for a second.

"Vaguely."

"We met right here, late last night. You were with your friend. It was right before Pele came over."

She dropped her chin slightly and screwed the top back on the water bottle. She took it and lifted her skirt slightly and wiped off the bottle. I kind of noticed that.

"It was late. I'm sure I'll remember." She paused for a second before she continued. "You played basketball late at night, here? Goodness, white boy."

"Please, call me Tim."

She looked at me, more like an inspection. I shifted from one foot to the other, self-consciously. The day hadn't become any less hot. The heat broiled Cranston Street. I saw shimmers of heat rising up from the asphalt. They wafted in flowing waves behind Sherri, framing her with waves of light. It almost looked like what a mirage was supposed to look like, except I had never actually seen a mirage. It gave Sherri a phantasmal, other-worldly quality. I shook my head like I had seen a vision and I needed to straighten out my understanding of it. Sherri noticed.

"What are you shaking your head about?"

"Nothing."

"Well, I am not nothing."

"I'm sorry. This is the first time I've spoken to a black girl."

"Really? For real? They don't have any black people where you live?"

"They do. Just no black girls, leastways none that I've spoken to."

"Black women."

"Huh?"

"Black women. I am not a girl. I'm a black woman."

"I'm sorry. Black women. I haven't spoken to none of them either."

I guess she thought that was amusing because she put her hand up to her mouth again and laughed long and hard.

"Good lord, man. You are a hayseed. That's for sure."

"Hey. Wait a minute. I'm just being honest. I don't know any black girls...ah, women. Cut me some slack, will you?"

Now I laughed a bit. Something about her, so foreign and exotic to me, disarmed me and made me less nervous, maybe like I should have known her my whole life, but I didn't, and I wanted to make up the time. It made the muscles at the back of my neck relax but put a twist to my stomach like I was opening some door that hadn't been opened yet and no one had seen what was on the other side. I kind of felt like I might throw up.

"You alright? You look a bit flushed. Would you like some more water?"

She held out the bottle and I took it quickly this time and downed most of it and held it back out to her without looking at it. This time, she screwed on the cap without wiping it off with her skirt. Now I laughed.

"Sorry about that. I just got all warm there for a minute."

"Well, it is about noon on Cranston Street in the summer. What did you expect it to feel like?"

"I guess not like this."

She looked at me some more and then shifted her weight again like she was scrutinizing some bug she found interesting. I wished I hadn't said, "I guess not like this" so quickly because I know I'm stupid, but the way it came out seemed like there might be a second meaning to what I said, and she was puzzled over why I said it. She waited a bit longer before she spoke.

"You planning on running again tonight?" She motioned across Cranston Street to the hoop courts that lay vacant at midday.

"I want to. I don't feel like waiting for three hours to get in a game, though."

"Marcus make you wait that long?"

"He did."

"But you got in a game."

"I did."

"Then stop complaining, white boy."

She laughed again and turned quickly on her heels and strode off. I stood there stupidly and wondered where she was going and why I couldn't take my eyes off her as she swayed down the street. The light that bounced off the asphalt of Cranston Street kind of lit the silhouette of her legs as they moved through her floral skirt. I watched her until she got to the corner of the street and turned left. The feeling of nausea I had a few minutes earlier came back and I wondered about it as I put on my work gloves and headed back to finish cutting the grass. I shook my head again like a prize fighter just knocked silly. A disturbingly strange thought crept into my brain and I was trying to shake it out through my ears. It was thrilling and it was nauseating and it was horrifying, and as I pushed the lawn mower mindlessly through my Meme and Poppy's back yard, the only fully illuminated thought I had was how much I hoped to see Sherri again when, and if, Marcus let me run with his boys tonight on the courts of Cranston Street.

# Chapter 12

## Pools

I did not taste my grandmother's ham and bacon casserole at dinner that night. Poppy sat across the table and looked at me with a twinkle in his eye. He was a man of few words, but he communicated perfectly with me. He saw that I fidgeted in my chair and hardly touched my food, like he knew there was some place I had to be other than sitting with two old French Canadians.

"Some place you want to go?" He looked at me until I put my fork down and wiped my face with a paper napkin.

"I was thinking about playing ball again tonight."

"You played last night? I looked out across the street and I saw people playing. I couldn't see you."

"It took me a while to get in, Poppy."

I didn't tell him I was there for hours until a spot opened up and that's the only reason I got to play.

"What? Someone quit?"

I put down my fork and it kind of clanked on my plate where the remains of my Meme's casserole grew cold.

"How'd you know?"

"Why else would they let you play?"

"Maybe they thought I might be good."

Poppy looked at me sideways like he knew that wouldn't have been the reason I got in the game.

"And they knew you would be good?"

"No."

"So, someone must have quit."

He laughed like he scored a point.

"Ha."

"You hoping to play tonight?"

Meme kept her eyes on her plate and ate daintily with her fork.

"Yes, Meme. I'm hoping to play tonight."

"Will Pele be there?"

Her question hung in the humidity that draped the kitchen. I didn't look up from my plate. Finally, I glanced up quickly and then dropped my chin and placed a small amount of casserole on my fork and slowly brought it to my mouth. I bit down and chewed maybe twenty times, like I never do, and then tried to swallow. The casserole was now a dry lump in my mouth, and I had a hard time getting enough moisture in it to swallow. I finally made this audible gulp sound that made my Poppy look up from his plate. They both looked at me carefully, waiting for me to respond.

"How do you know about Pele?"

"Everyone knows about Pele," they said in unison, not hard like how bad he is, but like everyone knew Pele, like the edge of a bed that you always bump your shin into and then hobble around calling yourself stupid because you knew the edge of the bed was there and you somehow could not avoid it and still managed to bruise yourself.

"We knew his parents. His mother, Hazel, worked at the tool factory at the corner of Cranston Street and his father, Bo, was a teacher at Central High. They were good people."

Both of them grew silent.

"You used the past tense, Poppy."

"Did I?"

"You said they were good people. Not they are good people."

"They've been gone a long time."

"What happened to them?"

Meme dabbed at her mouth carefully with her napkin and set it down on her lap precisely. She smoothed out her long dress and crossed her ankles under her chair. She cleared her throat and then pivoted her chair so she could look at me, like whatever she was about to say was going to be hard for her and she only wanted to say it once.

"She left them."

I looked at her and she looked back at me with those amazing, thoughtful, translucent eyes. I waited for whatever she was about to say.

"Hazel was about thirty-five at the time. Pele was ten. They had a very happy home. Bo made good money teaching English and coaching track. Things were fine. They were an important part of the neighborhood and the people loved them.

One summer day, Pele's sister, Charise, drowned at the city pool at the far end of Cranston Street, over by the police station. She went under and no one saw her. The city had made cuts so there weren't many lifeguards to go around. When they cleared out the pool area at the end of the hour like they always do, Hazel called out for Charise but couldn't find her. She ran around the edge of the pool thinking Charise must have gone off to play with friends or buy some ice cream, but after calling out for a while and no one seeming to know anything about where Charise was, Hazel took a desperate look into the deep part of the pool and saw a dark shape at the bottom. She dove in, even though she couldn't swim, and managed to push Charise's body to the surface. Hazel came to the surface screaming, "My baby, my baby!" as she thrashed about, drowning. A lifeguard pulled her out. Hazel pushed the lifeguard away and raced to where Charise lay on the hot concrete. She grabbed onto Charise and slapped her face like she was trying to wake her up. The police showed up and tried to bring Charise back, but she had been in the pool too long and passed.

I was coming home from work when I heard this deep, guttural wail from behind the chain link fence that surrounded the pool area. Hazel held Charise like a broken egg. She held her daughter and rocked back and forth and people tried to help Hazel. When the police tried to take the body, Hazel swung at them wildly in her madness. I ran into the pool area to see if I could help. I saw Hazel holding Charise and the wailing broke my heart. I dropped to my knees and put my hand on Charise's heart, and I knew she was gone. Her face looked like a little child's face as it rested in a crib. It was peaceful and awful and if it wasn't so horrific, I would have said that Charise looked beautiful.

Finally, Hazel's body went limp and she fainted. The police squatted next to Hazel and tried to bring her around. The fireman who had just arrived checked on Charise, but everyone knew by then that nothing could be done. The paramedics took both of them to the hospital. The city couldn't afford many ambulances that summer, so they put Hazel in the same ambulance as her dead daughter. It was a blessing that Hazel was unconscious, riding in the ambulance with her baby. Just before the ambulance got to the hospital, Hazel woke and looked over and saw her dead daughter. She tore off the straps they put on her while she was in the stretcher to get at her baby, so the paramedics sedated her and brought her to one of the emergency rooms. Bo was teaching summer school when he found out. He ran out of Central High and sprinted the mile to the hospital, only to find his wife sedated in one room and his dead daughter down the hall. Bo collapsed on the hospital emergency room floor. The police helped him up and took him to a waiting room until the doctors could come in to tell him his wife was ok, but his daughter was dead.

Lost in all the confusion was Pele. He was playing basketball with Marcus when he saw the police and ambulance arrive at the pool. Sherri was by the pool and saw everything happen. She ran in her bathing suit to the park and found Pele. The three of them ran to the hospital and got there about the same time as Pele's father.

The funeral was surreal. All of Cranston Street attended. Many of the French-Canadian families that still lived nearby dressed up in black suits and dark dresses to pay their respects. It was a sea of black and white trying to help Hazel and Bo and Pele say goodbye to Charise. Hazel and Bo sat in the front pew with friends and relatives. Their anguish couldn't be contained and the pain of it overwhelmed the church. Pele sat in the same pew, but when everyone left the church and followed the casket, Pele walked behind his father and mother like he was a ghost. He didn't cry. His eyes looked hollow and distant like he hadn't truly accepted that his little sister was gone. I think that hurt your Poppy and me the most; how he seemed a phantom as he walked down the aisle following his parents and his sister. When we got to the grave site, the preacher made a last, final speech that had everyone weak from the pain of it all. Hazel would not leave the burial mound. She moaned and wailed and all of it was so dreadful it was hard to watch. Finally, Bo and his brothers had to carry Hazel to the limo."

"It was awful," Poppy took a deep breath and looked out the back window of his duplex into his tiny backyard.

"What happened to Pele?"

"No boy should have to go through the pain he endured. Within a year, his father was diagnosed with cancer. He went quickly, but it was a painful death. The cancer devoured him. Some said it might have been a mercy because he couldn't live with the idea that his baby girl was gone. Pele was at his bedside the day he passed. I saw him a few days after the funeral. He was a shadow of the young man he used to be. And then his mother died."

"His mother died?"

"She couldn't take any of it. When her husband passed, she dove into the bottle and got into drugs. Her family couldn't help her. Pele couldn't help her. She died of an overdose two years to the day her baby passed. They found her in an alley behind the armory. She had been dead for days."

"Pele lost his whole family?"

"He did. His only two friends who really stuck by him were Marcus and Sherri. They came by his house every day after his mom passed. But he was broken, and they couldn't fix him. He got into selling drugs. They say he killed the man running Cranston Street, although no one could prove it. Sherri was with him up to then. She was the best thing that happened to him, but when he got deep into dealing the drugs, especially the coke, she left him."

"I heard Pele say to Sherri last night that she was still his."

"I think Pele thinks so. She was the only thing that kept him in one piece when everything fell apart. But she couldn't stand the dealing of the drugs and the violence that came with it. She had to leave him. Marcus keeps his sister safe, but I don't know how long that is going to hold. Pele wants Sherri back and wants her to be his number one girl. She told me once that she almost broke down and went back to Pele. I think if she did that, she'd be dead soon. Pele is in too deep. He can't get out and Sherri knows it. He keeps trying to get her back. I hope that girl stays strong on this."

"He tried again last night, after we came back from playing ball." Poppy had remained mostly quiet during the entire conversation. But he jumped in now.

"You're a young man, and you do what you want while we are at work but stay away from Pele. There's not much life to him anymore. He doesn't see any life to anyone, except maybe Sherri, and maybe Marcus. He won't see you as a life. Stay away from that man."

"I didn't see him at the court last night when I got in the game."

"You didn't see him, but he most certainly saw you."

"I'm just playing ball."

"Is that all you're playing?"

"Yeah, just playing ball."

"Pele is almost ruined. But there's a tiny spark to him, but it won't take much to dowse it."

I put my hand on Poppy's shoulder and gave Meme a peck on her cheek. I took their plates away and washed them in the sink. I dried everything and placed them carefully in the cupboard. Meme and Poppy sat at the kitchen table and said nothing, and I left the kitchen. If I had brains, I might have let what they said sink it. I didn't.

When I was ready to leave to play basketball, I shut the front door quickly because I didn't want my grandparents keeping me from the game. I didn't want any more information about Pele or Marcus, or even Sherri. I ran down the front steps of the porch. Of course, Beauchamp was there.

# Chapter 13

## Evelyn

"Ain't learned your lesson about them coloreds?" I tried to ignore him as I looked both ways down Cranston Street. "Sometimes they eat you slow, like road kill picked over by ravens. Don't trust them." He spat out an extra-large stream of juice. It landed too close to me.

"Shut up."

I made a dead stop and turned back to Beauchamp like I was going to charge at him. He held his hands up in defense.

"Just saying. Picked over by ravens."

He laughed at me and coughed up some swallowed juice and spat that out too. I wanted to run up his steps and punch the cigar out of his mouth. It would have pleased me to slug him, but in that moment, I shrugged off the desire. I could hear a basketball making metronomic beats against the concrete. I turned back and looked across the park to where the games had already begun. I decided there would be another time for me to pop Beauchamp in the mouth, but it wasn't going to be at that moment. I had a game to play.

I saw an opening in traffic and darted across the street. A cement truck rumbled down Cranston Street. The old, melting, cracked tar quavered as the huge tires rolled and the cement mixer churned, ready to fix some new crack in the foundations of Providence.

I jogged past some people heading home from work. They carried lunch pails or grocery bags and their feet moved deliberately across the dust and grass and pavement of the Cranston Street Park. They made no eye contact with me as I jogged past. They had business of their own.

When I got to the chain links that surrounded the courts, it was still very light outside. The sun was only halfway down its constant course and the heat continued to be almost unbearable. Sweat-soaked players ran up and down the blistering courts. It was inconceivable that their basketball shoes, worn and scuffed and torn as they were, had not been liquefied by the oven of the concrete. Still, they played on, driven by some unseen force, goading them toward one more jump shot or one more steal or one more furious dunk. There was a smaller crowd than last night, but it was also earlier, and it was still too hot to sit on the metal bleachers that reflected the sun's rays, adding to the incredible heat of the courts. Many families had yet to eat. I sensed they'd be out later when the night cooled slightly and the tedium of their day faded.

I walked quickly to the corner of the court where yesterday I had tried to be invisible. Tonight, I wanted to be seen. I wanted the people at the court, the players and moms and dads, the kids and the dealers and the hustlers and the bums and the old guard to see that last night was not a night that would drive me off the courts. I wanted in.

I also scanned the courts for Sherri. Since that morning, the image lingered of her swaying in her dress as she walked away from me. I wanted her to see me play. At the time, it was a visceral feeling; detached from my consciousness but nibbling at my corners.

Then I saw Pele. He was sitting on the top row of the bleachers. He had on a black and gold hat with a big "P" on the front. It might have been a Providence College hat. He was dressed in a black and gold t-shirt that ran down the length of his forearms. He wore extra-long basketball shorts that ended mid shin. His basketball shoes were an absolute white; even whiter than my basketball shoes. The same five guys who were with him last night were draped around him, like moons orbiting a giant, threatening orb. In spite of the extreme heat, not a bead of sweat could be seen anywhere on Pele. His dark-blue tinted sunglasses sat high on his nose. His head swiveled slightly, surveying his domain.

So there were three things that nibbled at my corners: getting in the game and proving myself, seeing Sherri again, and the menace of Pele as he sat upon his throne looking down on what, presumably, he knew to be his court. At that moment, I wasn't sure what was most important to me. The notions played on the outskirts of my thoughts and gnawed at me. I took my hand and swatted it across the air around my face like I was trying to get rid of a pesky bug intent on biting me.

I paid my dues and stood there silently and waited for at least an hour before Marcus called for me to run. Tonight, Ray and Leon and Henry had teamed up with Marcus, so when Marcus motioned me onto the court, I had a semblance of familiarity with his team. Tonight, however, instead of being dispatched to cover the opposing team's weakest player, Marcus set me to guard Albert. I thought Marcus was good. Albert was great. He said nothing to anyone on either team. His mute approach to the game contrasted with his magical flair. I had never seen anyone like him. He had a strong handle, his feet were invisibly quick, and he had the jump shot of an assassin. He did what not many players did anymore; he hit one mid-range jump shot after another. It wasn't flashy, but it was effective, and it was clear why Marcus put me on Albert. It was a test I had to pass. I was given the respect of being beckoned into the game. It was up to me to earn the respect of the court by accepting the humiliation of playing against the best player on Cranston Street.

The embarrassment could not have been more complete. Albert broke my ankles, got me off my feet, faked me one way and came back and hit an easy layup going the other way. I felt like I was in a different spatial dimension watching myself be played by Albert as the master puppet master. There were whoops from the players on my team every time I got schooled, and whoops from the opposition and the old men in the stands and the little girls who followed their daddies to the park and the women dressed in their skimpy summertime clothes and the street vendors and cabbies and a few cops who came around to watch. Pele sat in the stands and observed it all with the nonchalance of a viper.

Albert was just about finished toying with me when, as I bent over to put my hands on my knees in an act of full and complete defeat, Sherri arrived. She didn't so much walk onto the concrete surrounding the court; she seemed to be suspended above it.

Even in my state of exhaustion, I could see that she was the center of attention of everyone. Marcus nodded at her. Ray folded his chest and lifted one of his eyebrows. Henry's arms dropped down impossibly toward the court, but he tried to keep his shoulders straight. Leon held the tiny ball in his massive mitts and stood with his jaw agape. I straightened up and tried to look like I had played well which, of course, I knew she had seen me getting embarrassed by Albert.

She strolled over to the bleachers and elegantly placed herself at the very bottom, almost directly in front of Pele and his leering entourage.

"You boys going to run or stand there looking stupid?"

She laughed when she shouted this out and we broke from our trance. At this, Pele allowed himself the tiniest of smiles. He had to readjust his shades because the disruption in his appearance relocated his shades down his nose infinitesimally, and Pele could not have that. He took his arms off his chest and adjusted his shades and resumed his imperial pose. His buddies had sweat stains everywhere, but Pele remained without any hint of perspiration, in spite of the intensity of the Cranston Street furnace.

Marcus took the ball up court. I took a spot in the left side of the court, about eight feet from the baseline. Albert guarded me. He continued to be silent, looking forward to his next opportunity to shame me. I was kind of sick of it, and maybe Sherri's arrival sent a spark of adrenaline coursing through me, but as Marcus dribbled behind his back and toward my side of the court, I sensed that Albert was distracted. I'm sure he thought me inferior. It might have been how Sherri's entrance had focused his attention from me to her. I didn't know, but I was done being humiliated. I stood rather nonchalant, scratching the back of my head, looking disinterested, but as soon as Marcus looked my way, I bolted toward the basket. My backdoor cut caught Albert off balance. Marcus rifled a pass to me that I collected with both hands. I took one powerful dribble to the basket. One of Albert's teammates reacted, exploding upwards to swat my layup.

Since I'm not tall, this had happened to me many times. I coiled my body like I was beginning my layup, but instead of going up, I took one extra dribble and drove up and under the basket, using it to fend off the guy wanting to swat my shot. Instead, I drove up directly under the basket, cradled the ball with both hands about waist level, then swung my right arm up and flicked my wrist. The ball bounced off the other side of the backboard. It spun counter clock wise and settled perfectly into the chain-link netting. The crowd that had gathered was now at least one hundred. They were hushed and perhaps stupefied as I ran back to my side of the court. Marcus kind of glanced at me when I ran back. Leon stood motionless on defense, his colossal form almost blocking out the illumination from a nearby flood light. His jaw was agape as I ran past. There was a buzz from the crowd as I settled in my defensive stance, waiting for Albert to come up court. He looked amused, like it was dumb luck that he got beat. Something about the restless murmur of the crowd changed the way I had felt about the way I had been playing; the hush, in its own way, was more of a wave of applause then shocked indifference. My fuse was ignited.

Albert dribbled toward me. I could sense one of his teammates setting up behind and to my right. It was a classic pick and roll. Marcus had been pulling this trick on me all night. I was done with it. As he crossed over to drive past me, using his teammate to block me out, I darted to my right and using my left hand, flicked the ball away. No one pursued me. I figured they were too stunned. I took two long dribbles and drove my right knee up and made my second layup of the night. Now I ran back and the crowd was no longer quiet. They were rocking in the stands and along the sides of the court and outside, hanging against the rusted fence.

"White boy pick you clean!"

"Nice job, Albert."

"Who dat, Albert?"

The black people in the crowd gave Albert serious trash as I ran back. I felt the way I felt when I broke a long run in football or raced past someone on the track. I felt a palpable electricity surrounding me. This is what I experienced when on the courts of West Beaumont with my pals and knowing that I belonged. It was instinctive and thrilling and at the same time, there was a certain absence from my body. I was no longer a thinking, ponderous player. I was one with the game. It didn't happen all the time when I played any sport, but I knew it when it was happening, and without a doubt, it was happening tonight. I had entered what they called "the zone".

The game went on. Albert no longer beat me easily. He still beat me here and there, but there was a change to the way he played. Where he seemed to be in a complete zone just minutes before, he became tentative in his game, which of course is the one thing no athlete should do. Now, it was me who was juking Albert. I drove past him and bounced the ball between my legs to Henry who elevated and dunked. I stole a pass that was intended for Albert. I drove to the basket, this time passing the ball to Marcus. He received my pass in the corner, head-faked his defender, took one dribble to the baseline, and leaped into the night, making another of his impossibly high jump shots. With our team just a point from victory, Leon took a rebound and threw a bullet of an outlet pass to Marcus who quickly dished to me as I cut to the middle of the court. Albert went for the steal off of my dribble, but without the slightest bit of contemplation, I dribbled the ball behind my back, leaving Albert grasping at a ghost. I leaped to take my own jump shot, but Ray was wide open under the basket. Just when I reached the apex of my jump, I pulled back and rifled the ball to Ray who then jumped, caught my pass, and in one motion, deftly and gently kissed the ball off the backboard. The sound of it dropping through the chain netting sent the crowd into complete ecstasy. There was screaming and taunting and finger pointing and high fives and low fives and strutting. Money was being passed in the stands. Evidently, the betting against Marcus and the white boy was extreme. Swears showered down from the stands, but the money still got exchanged. The few guys in the bleachers who bet on my team had made a killing.

Both teams met at the middle of the court to shake hands or do that new hug where you shake hands and pull yourself in and bump chests, but of course, never look at the other guy. Eye contact on Cranston Street was rare; a commodity earned and not ever expected. When I got to Albert, we did the same thing. He stared at me for the smallest of moments, and then moved away mutely and swiftly and grabbed his gear and disappeared into the night carrying the unexperienced demon of being ass-kicked by a white boy.

I walked to where I hid my gym bag under the bleachers. I grabbed a towel from the bag and wiped myself off. I was a balloon floating in the searing night. I did not feel part of mortal, earthly bounds. I played very, very well.

When I took off my Pete Maravich game shirt, I looked up. Sherri sat on the bottom row of the bleachers. Her friend Evelyn had joined her sometime during the game. Evelyn looked at me with a strange smile. Sherri, on the other hand, was absolutely and completely making the effort to not look at me at all, which of course, made me think that maybe she had done plenty of looking. She sat with her legs crossed and fanned herself with part of a newspaper. I looked past her and up into the stands. There was Pele, motionless, eyes hidden by his dark shades. His buddies were settling up with the few people who had wagered for my team. Apparently, Pele was also in charge of the street hustle at the Cranston Street courts, and he was now paying up. He looked as deliberately away from me as Sherri had just done. I wasn't sure, but I thought I saw the tiniest bead of sweat just above his left eyebrow, illuminated by a flood light that shone off to the side of the court.

Marcus and Ray and Leon and Henry sat on the bottom of the bleachers a few feet away from Sherri and Evelyn. They had taken their shirts off. Their ripped bodies glistened. They used their shirts to towel off the profuse amount of sweat that had formed during play. They had no other shirts, so Marcus and Ray and Henry put them back on. The sweat made their shirts cling to their bodies. But Leon held his by his side like a rag. His musculature was indescribable. Every strand of muscle fiber flexed and relaxed as he moved easily and gracefully along the bleachers. I caught Marcus staring as well.

"Jesus, Leon. Put your shirt on. You embarrassing the rest of us."

"I can't help that I be bigger than the rest of you. God works in mysterious ways."

"You so big, you your own planet," Ray laughed. "You so big, you stupid."

The rest of us looked at Henry and then bust out laughing.

"Haw," grinned Leon as he sat on the bottom bleacher and flexed his chest and arms like a pro wrestler. "Haw," and Marcus and Ray and Henry bellowed and fell over each other.

I hadn't noticed that Pele had moved down with his entourage. Our delirium was replaced quickly with stillness.

"You cost me money tonight." He looked at first Marcus, then Henry, and Ray, and Leon, and finally his eyes settled on me. "I don't lose money."

"Well, you lost some tonight."

Marcus bent over and unlaced his worn, fully-black hoop shoes.

"Haw," grunted Leon.

"So, you running with my boys again, white boy?"

"Tim," I corrected him and then immediately regretted it.

He took off his shades and his eyes bored surgically into me. I backed off a few feet, which was also a mistake.

"Why you let him run with you, Marcus?" His stare never wavered.

"Kid can play. He passes the ball. Ain't many players do that on Cranston Street, 'cept Ray. And he don't like passing it much." Ray nodded his head and laughed again.

"What you say to that, white boy? You think you can play?"

"My name is Tim," I said firmly. "I played ok tonight."

I kept on making mistakes. Fortunately, there was a shift in the magnetic field and all of us turned in unison as Sherri walked over and stood next to Marcus. Pele put his shades back on, almost as if Sherri's aura blinded him.

"Nice game." She looked at Marcus and Ray and Leon and Henry in turn, but studiously did not look in my direction. "You sent Albert home mumbling, and that boy never talk."

She adjusted the weight of her body, with more weight on one side. She adjusted her head to one side and raised her eyebrow and made this smirk. She laughed a bit when she did it.

"And he don't lose."

The words came out of Pele almost without his mouth moving, like a snake flicks out its tongue sensing its surroundings. Pele's power was at once motionless and at the same time threatening, like a thunderstorm drifting down from Massachusetts. I imagined I could hear distant rumbles, yet the night around Cranston Street had become restlessly silent. There were things going on between Pele and Marcus and Sherri. Since I knew a little bit about Pele from my Meme and Poppy, the strangeness that I felt confused me because I felt like I was being pulled inexorably into their dark place. I didn't like it, but I stopped talking, probably the first good decision I made that entire day.

"So, I lost money. I'm making cheddar right now on the corner. What do you say, Sherri? Think much about what we talked about last night?"

"I ain't no one's woman. I said so last night. Nothing's changed." She said it with a powerful softness. The smoothness to her voice lent it purpose. It held Pele motionless. I found myself staring at her again, and it reminded me of what I felt that morning cutting grass. It was an inappropriate response to the situation, but it still made me nauseous.

"How about you, Evelyn? You ready to work for Pele?"

He said it in the third person and that always ticked me off back home. But I kept silent.

"I ain't dealing your poison."

She didn't say it with Sherri's power. Pele sensed the hesitation, and he moved toward her, coiled because of her hesitancy.

"I need a woman runnin' one of my corners. You'll do."

He said it to Evelyn like he had already made an executive decision, final and binding. Evelyn shook perceptibly. Sherri stepped in front of her. Marcus moved to Evelyn's side. Ray and Henry stepped closer. Finally, Leon lifted himself up and stood directly behind Evelyn. His vastness blotted out the evening stars.

"No one says no to Pele."

"She just did."

Sherri held her ground in front of Evelyn, placing one hand on her hip defiantly. Pele's buddies stepped down from the bleachers and stood behind him. My whiteness was insignificant and invisible. I shivered and hoped no one noticed my fear. Clearly, no one did. I wasn't even there.

"This ain't playing out right. But I see you won a game tonight and you happy about that, so I let it pass. But don't think we being friends once upon a time matter much now, Marcus. Those days long gone. I'm Pele now."

I felt the invisible barrier between both groups strain at the seams, like taut fabric about to rip. Now I did hear thunder moving toward Providence. It was just too hot, and the weather had to break. A lone charge of lightning illuminated the court. There was a slight pause before the crack of it. Someone or something had to give. I was surprised that it was Pele who took a step back.

"We talk again."

He looked at me once more; a hawk staring at its next meal. He and his buddies marched away and disappeared into the gloom that fully surrounded Cranston Street. I breathed. I must have been holding my breath the entire time because I felt the air rush in and out quickly and too loudly, I imagined, but no one paid me any attention. Everyone moved closer to Evelyn who continued to tremble. She was a mouse to Pele's snake.

"Let's get you home, Evelyn."

Sherri put her arm around her shorter friend. Marcus and Henry and Ray surrounded the two women. Leon followed, scanning the surroundings for danger. Another bolt struck, this time not far off. The jolt of the boom made me jump, but no one else reacted to it. They were in the middle of their own storm. I followed behind, unnoticed. A quick breeze picked up and rain began to fall, and the clouds overwhelmed whatever elation had permeated Cranston Street not minutes before.

# Chapter 14

## Stormy Weather

The rain fell hard. We held our hands over our heads like that might help. We were drenched by the time we ran down the street past my Meme and Poppy's duplex. A single light shone out from their living room. My Poppy must have been watching the Red Sox game. I don't know why at that moment I didn't say my goodbyes and run up the stairs of my grandparents' porch. I just didn't. Again, I don't think Marcus or Sherri or anyone else even noticed that I followed as they ran through the storm, turning this way and then that way until I lost all sense of bearing. Finally, they spun in a new direction and sprinted around the back of another duplex. Leon grabbed at the handle of a rusted bulkhead leading down into the darkness of a basement. He held it open and another lightning bolt lit up Providence. Everyone ran down the steps. It was only then that Leon noticed I was still with them. He was about to close the bulkhead door when he noticed me, rain cascading down my hair and over my face and chest and down to my skinny ankles. He held the bulkhead door open and let me come downstairs.

Instead of a musty basement smell, I was met by a sense of cleanliness. I expected maybe an old, run-down basement. When Marcus flipped on the lights, I saw a really pleasant, well-kept furnished basement, complete with a couple comfortable, firm couches, some easy chairs, and colorful drapes that covered the basement windows. It was altogether unexpected. This was Providence, so the basement should have been rotting away and filled with broken down furniture and molding boxes, and rats, lots of rats, but it was as properly furnished as any finished basement back in West Beaumont.

"Nice."

My voice startled everyone but Leon. They turned and looked

baffled.

"What you doing here?"

Henry had slumped down on one of the easy chairs, his legs sticking out almost half way across the basement floor.

"Yeah. We thought you went home, white boy."

Ray sat on one end of a couch. His arms were folded against his massive chest. His biceps strained against his soaked t-shirt.

"Tim," I said as I pulled my towel out of my gym bag.

I used the towel to mop off my soaked head.

"Let him be. He's welcome."

Marcus sat next to Ray.

"Get your slimy, soaked, old rattily bodies off these couches." Sherri put her hands on her hips and yelled it out. Her voice took up the entirety of the basement.

"Damn fools."

She laughed in a mocking way and ran upstairs. In a moment, she came back with a bunch of towels and t-shirts.

"Dry yourselves and change into these, you filthy animals."

She tossed everyone clean towels and some of Marcus' t-shirts. She helped Evelyn pull off her blouse. I blushed when Sherri exposed Evelyn's bra. I tried to turn away too quickly, which of course cracked everyone up.

"White boy never see no black woman's boobs?" Sherri laughed as she toweled off Evelyn and then helped her into a long, dry, striped blouse.

Evelyn's head popped through the top and she looked at me with no semblance of shyness. She might have minded that I saw her enormous breasts, but it didn't show. She might have blushed, I'm not sure. I wasn't aware that black people blushed.

Everyone finished drying off and found places on the couch or easy chairs. The last person to sit down was Leon. Marcus had given him an enormous robe that strained against Leon's considerable frame. He moved to the end of one of the couches. He looked down at Henry and Marcus. They sat there for a moment, like they had no intention of moving, but then slid quickly to the other side of the couch so they would not be squashed by Leon's wideness. When he sat, his side of the couch groaned under the stress of his bulk. I could see that where he sat on the couch, the springs underneath almost touched the floor.

"That didn't go too well with Pele."

Marcus slouched down on the couch and looked at Evelyn.

"I ain't selling his shit."

"He's trying to make you do it because of me. You heard him the other night. Thinks he own me." Sherri got off an easy chair and sat on the floor by Evelyn's feet and began to carefully massage her friend's legs. "He's using you to get to me."

"He ain't touching you."

Marcus leaned forward so he could look in Evelyn's eyes.

"How you going to protect me?"

Evelyn started to tremble again.

"I know him. He's twisted, but he wouldn't hurt you. He's damaged a lot of other people. Not you. He understands you with me."

Marcus' words calmed Evelyn down a bit. Leon reached up and pulled the string on one of the overhead light bulbs. The room became mostly dark with just the one light shining from the corner of the basement. Everyone in the room became very quiet. I sat on the edge of the steps leading upstairs. The room pulsed with low tension. I felt it. I thought I had begun to comprehend what it must be like to be black and live near Cranston Street in Providence.

"Such reckless hate." Sherri spoke quietly. No one looked at her. "There ain't nothing in Providence but reckless hate. I hate the fear we live with, and I hate that we know it ain't going nowhere. We get up and we work, and we try to live, and you guys get to play basketball at night and have people cheering you, and Evelyn and me work all day and come home and watch it all. We ain't got that. We just get argued over by assholes who think they own us or think we need to be protected."

"So, we don't play ball so you feel better about yourself? Is that what we supposed to do?"

Leon spoke with a deep rumble. Something surprised me about how he seemed to understand the complexity of what Sherri seemed to be saying. I don't know why I felt that way. Large means stupid?

"No, and since when did you or Ray or Henry or Marcus worry about having to give up the game? You think Evelyn and me have any say over what a black man wants to do? I'd be a fool for even thinking you giving up your precious game of basketball is ever going to happen."

"It's going to get me out." Leon's rumble became even more pronounced because it sounded so contained, but clearly, his emotions snuck out when he said it. "My daddy be my AAU coach when he not working as a tool maker. Says this is his ticket. Now I stop playing to make you feel better. Haw!"

What else surprised me was the fact that these friends spoke with me sitting right there. It was like I was being given a window into an obscure world. Here were good friends talking about problems just like I talked with my friends about problems. It was the same in West Beaumont as it was in Providence. I kind of laughed out loud at the realization. Marcus turned his head and looked at me.

"What you laughing about?"

I sat for a moment before I spoke.

"Just that I talk with my friends about my problems just like you are talking about yours. I think that makes us the same."

"Makes us the same. That what you think? We the same?" Marcus stood up. His extraordinary afro brushed close to the top of the basement ceiling.

"Sure, why not?"

"You think you like us because you can play hoop and we let you hang with us in our basement and we let you listen to us talk?"

I was going to speak but something told me to shut up, like I had stepped onto a rickety bridge that wouldn't hold up my weight.

"What your problems? Huh? What you worry about day and night back in West Beaumont?"

Marcus stepped closer to where I was sitting on the stairs.

"You worried about what time your mama setting dinner on the table, and whether she use the china or just the regular plates? You worried about whether your pool is clean? You worried about what college you going to? You worried about your SAT's? Those your problems? You worried about your pearly white Converse All-Stars getting smudged up playing with the niggers?"

I sat rigid on the steps. The rickety bridge was breaking.

"You don't know us."

"I'm trying to know you."

"You ain't ever going to know us."

"So, tell me."

"All you need to know right now is I'm not sure why I'm letting you sit here."

"I just wanted to play."

"Well, we let you in the game. We needed you. That was all there was to it, nothing more."

He stared at me and looked right through me. I was so clear to him, but he was so unfathomable to me.

"So, this is it."

He kind of nodded his head at the rest of the people in the basement.

"You see Pele and what he all about. You see Evelyn. You see Ray and Henry and Leon and my sister. What you see when you look at us?"

"I see you."

There was a long silence as everyone in the basement looked at me. I waited and adjusted how I sat on the basement steps and felt the bridge begin to splinter.

"That bullshit. You don't see me unless you be me. You know you gone by the end of the week. You get to leave this all behind. Back to Boston, or West Beaumont, or where ever it is you live. So why don't you take your white ass out of my basement?"

Marcus' voice raised an octave. Leon sat up and moved to the bulkhead door. He opened it up and stood aside to let me out. I continued to sit on the stairs until the strain of sitting became unbearable. I stood and moved off the stairs and grabbed my gym bag with my white shoes inside and I moved to the door where Leon stood. I looked back and saw black faces glowering at me, inflexible in their power. I looked to Sherri and her eyes looked like everyone's eyes. I had hoped she would defend me, but that wasn't happening. I turned away from her and looked up the stairs leading out of the bulkhead.

The storm had long since faded and the faint light of morning lit the exit. I pushed past Leon as carefully as I could and I climbed up and out and shivered in spite of the deep heat of the early morning. The door slammed shut behind me. I heard the latch of the bulkhead get turned and I knew I was locked out. I stood outside and looked around and saw rows and rows of tenements that made up the projects of Providence. The only places I had seen since I came here was my Meme and Poppy's duplex and the park and basketball courts across the street. I did not see the tenements when we ran last night through the thunderstorm and the downpour and away from the fear of Pele. I felt dull inside, like I was an empty can of beans. Marcus' words had cut me. I opened my mouth to say what I thought when I looked at everyone in the basement and Marcus went and shut my mouth. I was a dick to say, "I see you," and maybe I was a dick back home when I thought I understood black because I had two friends who came from black places. A stupid dick.

I looked around in the early morning haze. I saw wretched dogs in backyards digging through over-flowing trash cans. I saw dilapidated tenements that hadn't been painted in years; rotting wood holding up short stair cases that led to apartments with shattered windows. I saw bent roofs on tenements that sagged and buckled and cried out where shingles bowed. I saw an old, wrinkled man in what remained of a soldiers uniform squatting behind a dumpster. He took some newspaper from nearby and wiped himself. He walked off with his pants hanging off his emaciated frame. He was filthy and I could smell him from where I stood. I saw a young woman, no older than me, sitting on her porch. A baby suckled at her breast. She was as thin as the old, broken soldier. I wondered how she could feed her baby being that emaciated.

I moved through an alley that led between Marcus backyard and the tenement next door. Each of the tenements was about four stories tall. Just a few of them had front doors. The rest were unprotected from the uncaring of their winters and the intensity of their summers. There were no air conditioners in the windows; just fans that moved only because the hot breezes oscillated their blades. I saw people beginning their desperate days and moving where they were going to go or sitting where they were going to sit and still be sitting there for the rest of the day. I felt hot in the head and my stomach began to contract and I found myself running back behind the same dumpster where the old soldier just wiped himself. I retched unexpectedly, not far from where the soldier left his soil. I heaved again and again, and if I was home, I know my father would run to help me, but I was utterly and entirely alone with the sickness that spewed out of me. No one saw me heave my guts out. I remained invisible to the black families who lived in the dilapidated tenements that surrounded me.

I tried to wipe the bile off of my face and my t-shirt and my gym shorts. My only thought was to grab my bag and run in what I hoped was the direction that would lead me back to the ugliness of Beauchamp and the safety of my Meme and Poppy's duplex. I picked up speed, and even though I felt like I might puke again, I sprinted down Marcus' street and looked frantically for a sign that said "Cranston." I passed one side street after another. I became disoriented and began to panic. More people came out of their buildings and they looked at me and it terrified me even more. I felt the airlessness of the city and the neighborhoods and I was claustrophobic as more and more shadowy faces stepped onto the streets or out behind buildings or trudged up the stairs of buses. Finally, being completely lost in every way imaginable, I changed directions to sprint down another street. As I made my turn, I slammed full-speed into a light pole. My brain became disconnected and I found myself staggering along the street. My eyes rolled back in my head and the ringing in my ears became deafening. The stars that appeared in front of me blotted my vision and I swirled, and I began to collapse. I had no use of my limbs so my fall could not be broken. My head slammed into the impossibly hard and dirty and cracked concrete, and I felt the universe slowly swirl away to nothingness.

# Chapter 15

## Beauchamp

It must have been mid-day when I came around. I sat up and black people continued to walk past, ignoring me, or if they did look at me, it was a quick glance and a swift walk away. I smelled of puke. My shorts and t-shirt and sneakers were still wet from last night's rain, but they had shrunk and now were skin tight, so I looked like someone who hadn't eaten in days. My skull throbbed and I had a difficult time distinguishing shapes. Slowly, my vision cleared, but the ringing in my ears persisted. Once again, the heat of Providence stifled my breathing and I could see sweat mix in with salt from my perspiration from last night's game.

"You look like you've been eaten."

I heard a voice behind me and inhaled the familiar smell of a foul, chewed-up cigar. I picked myself up gingerly and turned and looked into the hideous, disgusting face of Jean Beauchamp. I blinked a few times to make sure it was him.

"Like rats eat garbage."

Beauchamp was about my height. He wore suspenders that kept his pants up over his skinny butt and immense belly. I could see a sliver of flesh sticking out between his stained t-shirt and his pants. I thought he stunk. And then I realized it was me who stunk.

"No one helped you up, eh? Did you think the coloreds would?"

I didn't have an answer to that, so I readjusted my t-shirt and tried to wipe away some of the retch from last night.

"What are you doing here?" I spoke groggily like I was listening to someone else.

"What am I doing here? I would ask the same thing of you."

He took his omnipresent cigar out of the hole in his face and held between the index finger and thumb of his right hand and shifted his weight to adjust the bag he held in his left. It looked like a grocery bag, which surprised me. Beauchamp ate? He spat tobacco juice straight down on the ground. Some of the spittle splattered on his work boots, the toes of which were greenish-brown from years of sputum.

"I think I got knocked out."

"Why else would you be here, sitting on the curb, coloreds all around, or were you buying drugs?"

"I wasn't buying drugs."

"Then why are you here?"

"I got lost early this morning. I couldn't find Cranston Street. I think I panicked, and I remember slamming into a light pole. No one helped me."

"Why did you think anyone would help you?"

"I thought they just would."

"You've been in cities before." He spat again. "You've seen coloreds before, some doing what you just did: lying in the street."

"This is different."

"Why is your situation different?"

I looked at him. He was disgusting. His skin hung off his face. He had a dark blue shade of a beard. His eyebrows stuck out at me. They couldn't have been trimmed in months. And his eyes had a recessed, hollow look to them. Right along his right eye and crossing over his eyebrows and just below his scalp, I could make out what looked like a long, jagged scar. It was swollen pink in the heat of the day as his face warmed and his body reacted to the swelter.

"I thought someone might help me."

"Why? When have you helped?"

I steadied myself again as a wave of dizziness passed over me. I thought about what he said. I had seen homeless people, mostly black people, when I visited Boston, but some white, and they always bothered me. I purposely tried to avoid walking anywhere near where they sat or wandered or panhandled. I didn't want to have to make eye contact or speak with them or anything. I wanted them not to be there. Thinking on it, I realized that when I was anywhere other than West Beaumont, I reacted the same way to all black people. I avoided them.

"Do you think you are the only white person they've seen on the street?"

He put the cigar back into his mouth and clamped down. A bit of juice squirted into his mouth and he swallowed it.

"White folk come in to Providence all the time. They buy their drugs. They usually leave and get stoned somewhere else, somewhere where they know there is money in case they want more, but some can't wait. They get stoned or O.D. and they pass out right here on the street and even die on the street and people walk by them all the time and they don't do a thing to help. Why would you be different?"

"But I didn't take drugs."

"Don't matter. You were lying there. Most people rather ignore than stoop down to help. Most people do what most people do."

He stood there and looked down at me, even though we were the same height. I shivered, even though the heat was ferocious.

"Cranston Street is this way."

He turned and moved off. I put my head down so no one could see my face and I followed behind. I was a lost animal. I wanted to be home.

Beauchamp turned right, then left, then left again, and I could see down the street the familiar row of duplexes and the basketball courts of Cranston Street. I walked behind Beauchamp, mostly because I didn't want to be seen with him. Black people scurried out of his way or tried to cross the street before he got to them and no one looked him in the eye.

As the heat became almost unbearable and I felt weak from no food or water, we passed where some of Pele's people sat on benches in front of the same liquor store where I saw them accost Sherri and Evelyn a few nights ago. Pele wasn't with them, but that didn't make me any less fearful. They leered at Beauchamp and then spit when I walked past, but aside from that, they left us alone. Maybe they didn't have marching orders from Pele to do anything to anyone unless he gave them specific instructions. Our showing up at that moment was unexpected to them, and like ants, they were directionless.

Beauchamp walked up the flight of stairs to his front porch, and surprisingly, I found myself following. He took out a set of keys that was attached to his pants by a thin, metal wire. Holding his bags in his meaty left hand, he slid the key in and turned the lock to his front door with his right. I noticed that his right hand was deformed; it looked like part of it was missing. He only had three fingers. His ring finger and pinky were absent and a chunk of the meat of his hand was gone.

I stepped carefully around the spittle from his tobacco juice that soiled his porch and I followed him inside. I walked as quietly as I could and said nothing. I didn't want to go to my Meme and Poppy's duplex yet. I was terrified of what they were going to say. They must be out of their minds with me not coming home last night. Still, I wasn't ready to see them.

When I entered Beauchamp's living room, I was startled to see that it was wonderful. Beautiful art work hung on the walls. His windows were splendidly clean. The view across Cranston Street was free of grime or dirt or any unwanted film. The drapes that hung by the window sashes were a rose-colored velvet with a maroon rope holding them in place. He had a long, dark-grey corduroy couch that had rose colored pillows on each end. He had one rocking chair that was situated so he could look out the front window of his duplex. The hardwood floors gleamed with polish. There was no evidence of dust or dirt or chipped wood or any other imperfection. He had a small TV with a silver antenna. It stood in the corner leading to his kitchen so he could easily turn on the TV or look out his front window. I stood kind of spinning in place like I had walked behind a curtain and seen the secrets that were hidden behind it.

Beauchamp kind of grunted for me to sit. He walked into his kitchen and I took a seat at the end of his couch. I heard noises like he was putting away his groceries, which still confused me. It never occurred to me that Beauchamp needed to eat. A cigar seemed like the only nourishment he took in, which of course, was ridiculous, but I couldn't see past the obvious visage of this disgusting man. And now I sat in his extraordinary living room and tried to sift through everything that happened to me last night and in Marcus' basement and now in this stranger's apartment. I felt wobbly again and closed my eyes to try to regain my equilibrium.

After a few minutes, Beauchamp returned. He was wearing green work pants. I was surprised to see that there were no cigar stains. He wore a button-down white shirt with short sleeves. The shirt had discreet blue lines and was what seemed to be clean cotton. He held a bottle of water out to me. I took it and unscrewed the cap, but my eyes never left him. He used the hand with the missing fingers to hold his own water bottle while his good hand twisted off the top. He deliberately lifted it up to his mouth and took a long drink. I could see the scar above his eyebrows move up and down as he swallowed his water. I sat for quite a while trying to comprehend the differences in what I was seeing from what I saw when Beauchamp was outside. I was utterly flummoxed over the contradictions between his completely repulsive outdoor appearance and the apparent neatness and orderliness of what was hidden within his duplex. He must have seen the look of surprise on my face.

"Not what you expected?"

"No."

I couldn't verbalize my thoughts since they were still muddled.

"Well, not everything is as it seems."

"But you're…"

"I'm what? Revolting? Is that what you were going to say?"

"I guess I was."

I said it too fast, but he didn't snap at me.

"I keep to myself."

He crossed his right leg over his left one. He took another sip from his bottle of water and studied me closely.

"You with the coloreds last night?"

"I was."

"Marcus? His sister?"

"Yes."

"Were they what you expected?"

"Nothing has turned out to be what I expected."

"Me included?"

"You included."

My eyes strayed to the scar above his eyebrows.

"You noticed my scar? Not just the cigar in my mouth?"

"I'm sorry. I didn't mean to stare. Everything inside your place is, it isn't what it ought to be."

"Because I'm foul and disgusting and a racist?"

"I think so."

"You don't know me."

"People have been telling me that quite a bit of late."

I took my eyes off the scar and noticed not a single ash tray or spittoon or any evidence that he smoked at all. My head still ached, and my ears continued to ring, and Beauchamp confused the hell out of me. I stood up and looked around. There was art work that looked to me like some impressionist painting and surreal images of intertwined people and still-arts of florals. His rug was intricately twined like it might be Persian. His coffee table was cherry wood with fine engravings and patterns. His wall clock was the kind without numbers. I walked over toward the kitchen. Next to his couch and across from his rocking chair were two photographs in clear glass frames. One was a picture of a young man holding a rifle standing next to other young men holding rifles. They wore the distinctive camouflage uniforms of the marines. My dad was a marine.

The second picture was a wedding photo. It was black and white with a hazy border, probably done on purpose. The frame was of polished gold. The woman looked sturdy; perhaps a few inches shorter than the strapping man in dress uniform, like the picture of my dad when he received his commission. I picked up the framed picture. It was the visage of a young Beauchamp with a wife. She sat on a chair and he stood behind her. They smiled deeply and completely. I looked at it for a bit. The picture of Beauchamp with a woman puzzled me. How could anyone love a man like Beauchamp? I carefully replaced the golden picture frame and turned back to look at Beauchamp. He sat patiently, which also confused me. I expected him to spit.

"That's my wife and me. 1955. Got married right after the war. Moved here in 1956."

I just stood there in my skin-tight t-shirt and shorts and walking around basketball shoes and my confusion deepened.

"You didn't expect this."

He made a sweeping gesture encompassing his living room.

"I really didn't."

"Like I said, not everything is as it seems."

"Why stay here, Beauchamp? You hate these people."

"Much of the time."

"Then why stay?"

"I can't leave her. The coloreds think I'm crazy and a racist bastard and they're probably right, but I can't leave her."

"Your wife."

"Yes. I came home from Korea. You know Korea."

"Some."

"Korea. I was a young man and I didn't have a job. I enlisted when the war broke out. Thought I was fighting for something."

"You weren't?"

"I thought I was. Then my division got sent up north, over the border. Chosin."

"Chosin reservoir?"

"The Chinese came at us in waves in the bone-snapping cold. They just kept coming. They wore rubber sneakers so they could get close to us and we wouldn't know they were there until they were among us. We fought with frozen hands and feet and we were still wearing our summer gear."

I sat for a moment and looked out his front window.

"I killed men. I watched friends die. We retreated and I stumbled through the ice and snow. We were being pursued by the Chinese and under constant attack. I remember seeing a sudden flash and a loud explosion. I didn't remember anything else until I woke up in a hospital tent. I was there for a month, then they moved me to Tokyo, and I stayed there for another month. The Chinese gave me this." He held up the hand with three fingers. "And they gave me this." He took his good hand and ran has index finger along the scar above his eyebrows.

"I came home. I was lost. There weren't any parades or testimonials for the soldiers. I don't know if America cared or even knew we were home. My family lived in Quebec and they were poor, so they had a hard time coming to visit. I wandered through Southeast Massachusetts. One day, I found myself in a church. They had a soup kitchen. I was starving, so I went in. She was there. My Genevieve. She helped serve sandwiches and ladle soup. To this day, I have no idea why she picked me. But there she was.

We got married. I found a job working the railroad. She was a nurse. We left Fall River and moved to Providence because I got a promotion at the Boston and Maine Railroad and Genevieve got a job in the ER at Rhode Island Hospital. We were good. We saved up and bought this house a few years later."

Beauchamp looked down at his polished floor. He was in a different place and time. I let him be.

"She was walking home from work. We were expecting by then, maybe three months out. The car came around the corner. She never saw it before it ran her down. They brought her to the same hospital she worked at, but they couldn't save her. Ironic, really. The police came to the railroad to let me know. They said she died calling out for me. The police said some colored ran her down."

He got up and moved to the table and picked up the gold-framed picture. I looked at his eyes. They were eyes that saw everything and saw nothing, and he was empty.

"I kept working. More coloreds moved in and the whites moved away."

"Why did you stay?"

"Genevieve's home. She turned it into something beautiful; something beyond my understanding of joy and forgiveness and relief. I thought Korea would never leave me, but she found a way to get inside of me so I could get outside of me."

He put the glass-framed picture carefully back where it sat. He adjusted it so it was perfectly lined up so he could see it from his rocking chair. He moved away slowly and put both hands on the arms of his rocking chair. He bent over and sat carefully, like he didn't want to disturb the thing that he just let out. I sat for a moment before I spoke.

"You are two different people. The one in here and the one that spits tobacco juice and mocks people as they walk by."

"The colored people."

"Yes."

"They killed her. Some drunk colored ran her down and killed her and killed me."

"I don't understand."

And I didn't. How could someone be so completely different outside compared to the person living within?

"They ran her down."

"You said the police told you it was a drunk."

"Colored drunk."

"Did the police say that, specifically, that it was a colored drunk?"

"They didn't have to."

"Even if it was, does that mean they all deserve your hate, because you do hate them. I don't know you, but I could tell you were filled with hate the moment I saw you spit at an old woman and a young girl. You're swimming in it. Why don't you stay inside if you hate them so much?"

"I am inside. What I show them, or your grandparents, or you," he raised his voice when he said this, "is all anyone deserves to see."

His words came from a deep, dark place, a place he had not or could not let go.

"You're not what I expected, Beauchamp. I think I'm figuring that everything I see here is filtered; you, Marcus, Sherri, even Pele. I can't see through you and I can't see through them. Everyone here is a stained window like you see in church where the colors are obvious, but you can't see through the glass."

I looked at him for a bit and he stared back. His eyes were like church windows. There were too many colors in the way.

I sat up and stretched and realized how hungry I was. I had to get over to Meme and Poppy's house and I knew it would be hard when I went there.

"I have to be leaving. My Meme and Poppy must be out of their minds by now."

"Probably."

I found my hand reaching out toward Beauchamp. He took it with his mauled, deformed hand and looked me in the eyes.

"Don't let the coloreds know."

Again, he gestured with his arm around the house. His words caused me to bunch my shoulders in anger, but I relaxed them quickly because I wasn't sure if I was mad at what he said.

"I won't."

We shook hands and I moved to the front door and left the cool of Beauchamp's unexpected home and stepped into the blast furnace of Cranston Street. I could see guys playing ball off in the distance at the park. I turned my head and saw Pele and his boys on the corner running business, but they didn't seem to see me. I jogged down Beauchamp's front steps and ran up Meme and Poppy's and the cars kept racing and people came home from work and the pulse and the desperation of Providence continued to throb.

# Chapter 16

## Ticket to Ride

Meme and Poppy sat shoulder to shoulder on their corduroy couch. When I stepped through the door, Poppy sprang at me. His quickness off the couch was startling. I put my hands up in defense as he swung at me. The meat of the palm of his right hand hit me upside my right ear. It renewed the thunderous pounding in my ears that had seemed to dissipate when I was at Beauchamp's. I bent over and grabbed my head between my elbows and a scream escaped powerfully. But that was all he did. He simply moved away and sat back on the couch with Meme. Where the pain from his slap was entirely physical, my Meme's stare bore into me and through me, and it dropped me to the floor more effectively than a smack to the side of my head. That's what my dad would do to me if I messed up back home: stare me to death. I sat there by the door with my feet pulled up to my chest and my ear throbbing and the dull ache of my concussion driving back against the inside of my skull. The quiet of the room was set against the slow tick-tock of an old clock that stood sentry over their living room.

"I'm sorry," I whimpered.

"What are you sorry for?" Meme kept her cold stare fixed on me. "Staying out, not calling, not coming home, or making us think you were dead, which one?" Meme's voice did not elevate. It didn't have to.

"We let you stay with us because we thought you were a man and would be respectful. You failed."

"Do you understand?" Poppy jumped in.

"I understand nothing."

My voice sounded outside of me; like some other entity was present in the room who was unfamiliar to me in every way.

Poppy thought I was being an ass. He got up off the couch like he was going to hit me on the other ear. I began to sob. He backed off. It was a while before I could regain my composure.

"I understand nothing about you, or the coloreds, or Beauchamp. I am completely screwed up by my lack of comprehension of this place."

When I was upset, I tended to use long sentences and big words. It usually got me out of trouble with my dad, so I figured it would work here. I failed again.

"Don't call them coloreds." Poppy paused for a moment. Then he picked up some papers that sat between he and Meme. "We're sending you home. Here's a bus ticket. You're not man enough to be trusted."

Poppy waved a Greyhound bus ticket at me. There was darkness to his eyes. Meme looked at me with disappointment. How could I tell them how sorry I was when I knew what I put them through?

They were right. I had to go home.

I spent the rest of the day and night trying to fall asleep in my tiny bedroom. When I did manage to fall asleep, it was fitful. I was soaked with sweat and the noises of the city kept me from falling asleep until finally, I was just too exhausted and passed out naked on the damp sheets. I drifted away and dreamed of rusted cars and broken windows. The dream was cinematic. Black faces swirled through city dust. Two giant duplex houses dominated the background. They both belched dark smoke that hung in the air. The bodiless black people coughed and choked and tried to cover their faces with their shirts or blouses, but eventually their faces were beaten down by the heat and the smog and the noise and the heaviness of the unrelenting swelter. I floated above them in the cool of a blue sky that was unreachable to them. They stretched up to me in a futile struggle to rise out of the tumult. They fell back into the shadows that consumed them.

I woke up. The sheets of my bed were strewn about my room like someone had broken in and stripped them off. I sat up and tried to wipe away the soggy sleep that caked my eyes. I listened for noises coming from outside my room, but Meme and Poppy's home was silent and lifeless. I looked at the clock and saw that it said 10:00 AM. They must have gone off to work. It was Wednesday. I was supposed to stay until the following Sunday. Now I knew that wasn't going to happen. I swung my legs off the bed. My ears seemed better, but my head continued to thump with pain. I stood up shakily and balled up the soaked bed sheets and dropped them into a hamper that sat in the corner of the bedroom. I opened the door and staggered to the bathroom where Meme and Poppy had a tiny shower that sat inside an old tub. I turned on the water and let it warm. I climbed in and let the heat of the water flow over me. I stunk. I took some plain soap from a dish and tried to scrub off the stench. I ran the soap through my hair and under my pits and around my crotch and down to my feet. Grime swirled in the tub and passed into the old pipes that led away from Meme and Poppy's house and into underground drainage and away to its final destination in the Narragansett River. Maybe the grime was cleaned away when the Narragansett River turned into the Narragansett Bay and swept it out to sea. Something told me that the water was no cleaner out there than it was in here.

I grabbed a towel that hung from an iron beam that ran down the length of the bathroom wall. I dried off. I found that the towel became dirty and realized that whatever I had done to wash away the filth had not been wholly successful. I tossed the no-longer white towel into the bathroom hamper and walked back naked to my little bedroom. I opened the tiny closet and pulled out clean sheets and a pillow case. I tried to make the bed as neat as it was when I moved in last Sunday, but I wasn't going to be able to do it as well as Meme had done it. I did what I thought was a good job, but then stood back and realized the bed still looked disheveled. I stripped it and tried again, and it looked a bit better. Maybe I just wasn't going to be able to replicate that which my Meme did with ease.

I found myself sweating again. I put on another pair of shorts and a clean t-shirt and some white socks that I tried to pull up to my knees. The socks were old, and when I pulled one up, the elastic top unraveled. I let the sock ball up around my ankles. I put on the other sock and didn't bother to try to pull it up. I put on the same sneakers I wore last night. They were dry now and were quite tight around my toes. When I finished tying them, I looked into my gym bag. My Converse All-Stars nestled perfectly in the deepest part of the canvas bag. I reached in and gently pulled them out. They were almost flawless. I held them gingerly like anything I did to them now would make them less perfect. It was brutally hot in my bedroom. I opened the window that faced out onto Cranston Street. I put the All-Stars back in my bag, zipped it shut, and left my room. I had to escape the heat.

I opened the front door and walked out onto the porch where there were two rocking chairs. I sat down in one of them and put my foot up on the railing. Cars and buses and taxis moved along. Black people walked where they were going to walk and went where they were going to go. The drone of the movements of the vehicles and the people made me drowsy and I felt myself drift off. I don't know how long I slept. Sometime later, I felt a bang on the porch. I was startled awake and looked around and saw that Sherri was sitting in the rocking chair next to me. She had kicked the railing of the porch to wake me up. The sun was dipping closer to the horizon and the beams of light almost blinded me. I took my feet off the railing and sat up straight like I would do if were horsing around in a classroom and a teacher walked in. Sherri saw how startled I was and laughed. My first thoughts were the images from the night before when I was tossed out of her and Marcus' family basement. I thought she was going to be pissed. She wasn't. Her eyes danced with amusement. I didn't know what to say, so I didn't say anything. I just sat there with my mouth hanging open and a look of confusion on my face.

"It's ok." She laughed when she said it. I still didn't know what to say so I continued to sit there, stupidly. "I see you made it back to your Meme and Poppy's house. Were they angry?"

"They're sending me home."

"Of course they are. You're an idiot for even being here."

She laughed out loud when she said it. Once again, just like the day before when I was cutting the grass, I found myself lost in the depth of her eyes. But now I felt a thread of danger. Pele owned this part of Providence, and even though Sherri had established her identity separate from Pele's, and even though I was an idiot, just like she said, I pulled back from the trance I let myself fall into and turned away. I looked off across Cranston Street to the courts and the games going on there and the people walking to and from work or whatever they were doing as the day started to end and the hum of early evening enveloped the city.

"I should have never come here."

"Why not? Because you not black?"

"Yes."

I said it a little too loud. Sherri took her rocking chair and turned it to face me.

"And you think we hadn't noticed?"

She cocked her head to one side and raised her eyebrows and crossed her arms. I sort of laughed.

"I don't' understand anything about this place. I don't understand you, or your brother, or Beauchamp, my grandparents, or Pele, really none of you." I looked at her and then dropped my eyes to the porch floor. I didn't like not knowing.

She looked at me, but said nothing, which in itself was a distinct message. Yeah, you don't understand anything. That fact was the only thing I think I did understand. Sherri and I sat there staring at each other for what seemed like too long a time when a sleek, dark car with spinning silver wheels turned down the far end of Cranston Street and toward where we were sitting. It slowed down ominously. Sherri turned her chair to face the street. She put both of her feet flat on the porch and gripped the arms of the rocking chair. I could see the pink of her knuckles through her dark skin and the flexing of her forearm muscles. Her jaw was tight, and a small vein pulsed along the side of her neck. The car continued on. Deep, booming music bellowed from inside. The car almost came to a stop, but never ended its menacing forward momentum, like a predator deliberately moving through its territory. I felt the muscles in my calves tighten and my neck begin to tense.

"Is that Pele?"

"No, he's down on his corner. That's someone else."

The car slowly picked up speed to where it was only moving as fast as the people walking by. From on the corner, I could see Pele and his buddies stand and look down in the direction of the dark car. It kept its threatening pace as it passed Pele, who was now stepping toward the edge of the sidewalk. His entourage stood directly behind him. When the dark car was level with Pele, he put his arms up with his fingers extended in a Jesus pose, like he was mocking them or standing in challenge. The car never slowed down when it drove by Pele, but someone in the car turned the music up even higher and the boom of the base beat thundered over to the park. When the car got to the lights by the street corner, it turned right and accelerated, laying rubber and a cloud of exhaust as it raced in front of the Cranston Street Armory.

Sherri relaxed her grip on the rocking chair and her feet slid out toward the railing of the porch like she had become completely drained in the few seconds it took the dark car to drive by. My calf muscles eased, and my neck relaxed, and I felt myself exhale since I must have been holding my breath the entire time the dark car stalked along. As much as Pele felt threatening to me, whomever was in that car created a more penetrating sense of dread. Pele and his guys walked toward us as the dark car disappeared. Their strut was full of confidence and bravado. If they were as terrified as I was, or Sherri, they showed no outward sign of intimidation. I understood that look. It's a look I tried to have playing basketball or football, even if I was terrified. I could hear the clicking of Pele's boots as he drew even with Beauchamp's duplex.

I hadn't noticed that Beauchamp had come out of his house and was sitting on his rocking chair, now wearing his familiar looking, disgusting clothes and sucking on a putrid-smelling cigar and spitting nonchalantly like he always did. Outward facades. Something caught my eye in the opposite direction. Evelyn strode toward us, cutting the distance between her and Pele in quickening strides. Her hair was pulled back and she wore a summer skirt and matching blouse. Whereas Pele and Beauchamp presented a visage of bravado, Evelyn looked rattled. Something must have startled her. She started jogging toward us. From behind her, I saw the same dark car. It must have made a lap around the Cranston Street courts and now turned and followed along the same route it had just traveled, but this time the car was accelerating quickly; engines roaring. When it drew close, I could see the backseat window roll down and a metallic object extend out from the darkness. Sherri let out a deep, horrified scream.

The car raced past. As it did, a flurry of pop, pop, pops burst out from a lone arm extending out from the back seat. Pele and his buddies either jumped onto the pavement or dropped down behind parked cars or raced toward the alley between Meme and Poppy's and Beauchamp's duplex apartments. Sherri leaped off her rocking chair and tackled me and drove me hard onto the floor of the porch. Chips of wood splintered around us and glass exploded at my bedroom window. More pops came from the car and then it raced away, running through the red light down where Pele and his buddies had stood just moments ago. Sherri kept pressing down on me, even though the gunshots had ended. When she moved off of me, I was able to jump up. The smell of cordite was heavy, and my ears rang severely. My eyes darted from side to side. As I surveyed the landscape, I could hear a low moan coming from directly in front of the porch, down where we could not see who was making that noise. I stood up and looked out over the railing. Evelyn was curled up, holding her stomach. A large, red stain spread across her summer blouse. Sherri joined me at the railing and let out a startled scream.

"Jesus, Evelyn!"

Sherri raced down the porch steps and over to where Evelyn lay on the baking sidewalk. She slid on her knees and gathered Evelyn in her arms. She held Evelyn's head in her lap and cried out in a way I had never heard before, like something primal and dark.

"I have you, baby. I'm holding on. Look at me, Evelyn. Dear sweet Jesus, look at me!"

She begged Evelyn to hang on. I had never seen anyone die before, never mind even getting badly injured, but something told me Evelyn was dying. Sherri's clothes were covered in blood. She had her hands pressed against Evelyn's stomach like she was trying to keep the life inside from spilling out onto the sidewalk. I could see perfectly down into Evelyn's eyes. The pupils were minute, and her eyes stared transfixed up into the late afternoon haze. Her chest rose and fell quickly, and she held tightly to Sherri, now adjusting her gaze to look pleadingly into her eyes before Evelyn's pupils began to lose their focus.

Pele had been flat on his face no more than ten feet from Evelyn when the bullets started to fly. He leapt to his feet, sprinting toward where Sherri held Evelyn. He slid across the concrete and took Evelyn from Sherri and gently tapped Evelyn's face like a father would do to a newborn that had too long of a nap. She remained motionless. He bent over and looked down into

Evelyn's now lifeless eyes. He didn't scream or cry out or moan. He just looked down at Evelyn. Quickly, he stood up and began to run down the street, carrying Evelyn in his arms. She flopped about, her head drooped over his right arm, his buddies scurrying out from their hiding places to join him.

Then I saw Beauchamp. He came running down his porch steps. He held a metallic-grey tool box. He stopped Pele with one hand extended onto Pele's chest. Surprisingly, Pele stopped his charge down the street and put Evelyn down. Beauchamp opened the tool box. That's when I realized it wasn't a tool box; it was an old medical kit. He opened it swiftly and took out a large wad of gauze and stuck it into Evelyn's waist where the blood seemed most extreme. He lowered himself to try to see if Evelyn was breathing. He took his index and middle finger of his three-fingered hand and checked for a pulse. He kept his fingers there for a while, perhaps hoping a pulse in Evelyn would resume. It obviously did not. He looked up at Pele who now stood above Evelyn. Pele's face lacked any form of expression, but his fists clenched and the muscles on the back of his neck bunched up on his shoulders. His buddies formed a circle around Beauchamp and Evelyn and Pele, all of them facing outward across the park and down the streets as soldiers do when fearing attack. Finally, Beauchamp picked up Evelyn and handed her to Pele. He turned and walked slowly down Cranston Street with Evelyn curled up in his arms and his crew walking almost in unison behind them.

Sherri remained seated on the concrete just below my grandparents' porch. It was now splintered with bullet holes. The window that opened to the little bedroom where I slept just hours before had been obliterated. The sash that surrounded the glass window now hung wildly and swung back and forth, held to the frame of the house by a single nail. I jumped over the railing and landed a few feet from where Sherri sat. I almost slipped on the pool of blood. I sat down next to Sherri and put my arms around her, and she began to moan and cry out and punch me in the chest until I held her tighter. She sobbed onto me. I looked around. There were a few black faces who had gathered after the drive-by. But soon they walked off and tended to their own affairs, as if this had nothing to do with them. A bus stopped a few houses down and Meme and Poppy stepped down along with a number of black people coming home to the intensity of the late afternoon. They moved this way and that. Some looked at me holding Sherri and the carnage of my grandparents' house and Beauchamp who now squatted next to us. His omnipresent cigar sat in the corner of his mouth, but he did not spit or curse. He simply squatted with his med kit and waited to see if he was needed. It was the first time there was a blend to the inside Beauchamp with what he chose the world to see.

Meme and Poppy took two steps away from the bus. They saw the carnage and rushed over as fast as elderly people can move. Meme kneeled down, and I could see her yellow shoes begin to stain from Evelyn's blood. Poppy stood next to Beauchamp and surprisingly put a hand on his shoulder. Beauchamp stood up, holding his med kit, and turned and looked at Poppy with tired eyes. Maybe the two of them had seen this kind of thing before. They were tired of it, and I still wondered why they stayed, with all of the threats and violence and butchery.

Meme helped Sherri stand and began to walk with her down the street. She kept her arms around Sherri like she was shielding her. They walked down the street and turned a corner and the city continued to breathe and basketball players continued to shoot jump shots and buses drove by and cars blasted their stereos and Cranston Street strained to stay alive.

After a few minutes, with me still paralyzed on the blood-stained concrete, Poppy came back out from his duplex with a mop and a bucket of water. He handed the mop and bucket to me and walked back into his shattered house. In a moment, he looked through the mangled window of my bedroom and using work gloves, began to pick up pieces of glass. I dipped my mop into the bucket and began to slop up the blood. The rich, deep, gruesome crimson of Evelyn's blood slowly began to fade to a diluted film of pink. I continued to mop and finally, when I thought the stain was mostly gone, I took the bucket filled with Evelyn's blood and I walked over to a sewer drain and dumped the bucket. It swirled down into the sewers of Providence and I guess flowed off toward the Narragansett River and the Atlantic Ocean where maybe it would dissolve with everything else that coursed through the rancid sewers.

# Chapter 17
## Late Day Bus

I was about to climb the stairs and return the slop bucket to Poppy when Marcus arrived with Leon and Henry and Ray. Leon stepped close to me and blotted out the sun. Henry stood erect with his hands drooped down to his knees. Ray stood, arms folded, expressionless, next to Marcus.

"My sister was here with you?"

"We were sitting on the porch."

"That's when Evelyn come by? And Pele?" Marcus appeared surprisingly calm; perhaps contained was the better word.

"They walked toward each other just when the dark car came down Cranston Street for a second time." I looked at Marcus and asked what I thought was obvious. "Were they trying to kill Pele? Was it somebody from another gang?"

"No. They were trying to kill Evelyn or Sherri."

Marcus moved away from me and paced up and down the sidewalk. He made sure to step around the damp spot where I had just finished washing out the now-drying blood stain. His containment began to ebb. Now there was clear agitation in his movements. He looked down the street in the same direction Pele had carried Evelyn. Henry reached one long arm up and began to massage the sinuous muscles along his neck. Ray's biceps bulged against his black t-shirt. I could see a faint semi-circle of sweat that had shone through. They gave Marcus space to pace back and forth.

I didn't get it. Why would another gang who had the opportunity to take out Pele purposely miss him but kill Evelyn and almost kill Sherri, and me for that matter?

"They must have been terrible shots."

It sounded stupid the moment it seeped out of my stupid mouth. Leon looked at me and frowned.

"You watch too many movies about blacks in the city. Whoever shot Evelyn wanted Pele to see it. Sent a message without starting a war. Now Pele either back off this corner or he take out someone close to them, and then it escalate."

Ray stepped forward.

"Might have been Raja from the South Side. He been wanting Cranston Street. Too many white boys and girls come here for drugs to ignore." He kept his arms folded over his bulging chest. "It ain't over." Marcus looked at Ray and nodded once in agreement.

"Sherri still in danger, Marcus." Leon's baritone voice came out mellow and soft. I didn't think the voice fit the situation. "So's Tim. He saw it, too. They know he saw it, they be back soon enough. What we do, Marcus?"

Everyone turned to face him. It might have been funny for someone walking by to see my eyes clearly bug out of my skull. Someone wanted to kill me?

"I don't understand. Why kill me? Wasn't Evelyn enough?"

"She was, 'cept Sherri got all bleeding heart on you, white boy, and she in the wrong place at the wrong time. Now they'll come after her. And you."

Marcus saw my horror at the change in the situation. He almost laughed. He clarified it for me.

"You nothing to them. Just some white junky hanging about. It might have confused them to see Sherri rocking with you on your grandparents' porch. Don't matter. You a bug. Raja gonna step on you."

"We got to get Sherri hid." Henry continued to massage his neck while he spoke. "But you know your sister going to Evelyn's funeral, whenever that be. You know your sister. There's no

111

getting around that."

"So, we put her in my basement and stand guard round the house until the funeral. Then we think of something else."

"What about Tim?" Leon took a step closer to Marcus. "Can't leave him. They come again, they take him out. Can't have that." Thank God for Leon.

"Screw them. None of these crackers belong." Ray nodded to my Meme and Poppy's duplex, and then over toward Beauchamp's, and then finally toward me. "And they ain't moving out on their own. Let Raja finish it."

Ray let his folded arms drop from his chest. I was too much of a coward to say anything. I felt my stomach begin to churn and I began to sweat more profusely in spite of the temperature having to be more than 100. My legs wobbled and I began to slide toward the concrete. Leon put out his meat of a hand and helped me steady myself. He seemed to be the only one remotely concerned about the fact that someone wanted to kill me. That's all I cared about: me.

I would have tried to save them if I was in their situation. I know I would. Of course I would. So, I thought they would want to try to save me too. The fact that Marcus and Henry and Ray weren't saying anything, maybe just thinking about whether I was worth it or not, made me feel like my fate was already decided. I looked at Leon and realized that his sense of commitment to keeping me alive was not overwhelming Marcus and Ray and Henry's lack of distress. They were worried about Sherri. I wasn't close to being their concern.

"Hide the colored girl in my basement."

While Marcus and Henry and Leon and Ray and me stood near the steps leading up to Meme and Poppy's porch, Beauchamp stole up behind us. We had heard nothing except the omnipresent sounds of Cranston Street. He just materialized.

"I'll hold the girl until this thing is worked out between you coloreds."

Beauchamp was in his late fifties. He certainly didn't look fit, yet he was able to steal up to us without us noticing, maybe like those Chinese soldiers moving in the dead of winter wearing basketball sneakers.

"Ain't your business. We take care of this." Marcus stepped closer to Beauchamp. "Keep your cracker ass out of this."

"I heard you talking from my porch. If you think you can keep your sister safe in your basement, you'll all be dead before the funeral."

"How you know that, Beauchamp?" Marcus spit on the ground.

His saliva landed a couple feet away from Beauchamp's tobacco-stained shoes. Beauchamp looked down at the spit but didn't move.

"I know Pele. I know of Raja. I sit on my rocker all day and listen to you coloreds talk and your world slides past mine and you don't think I hear. I hear Pele talk to his boys about Raja. He pretends he's not afraid of him, but I know better. Pele has done some awful things to a lot of people. He hates, and that's why he kills to keep his turf. Raja doesn't hate. He doesn't feel anything. He's a sociopath. He'll be looking for where you would hide your sister and he'll kill her and your family and your boys, Marcus. He won't think that I have your sister."

"So, a white man bailing out a black man?"

"If you think of it that way."

Beauchamp thrust his hands into the pockets of his dirty overalls in a kind of "take it or leave it" motion. Marcus looked at Beauchamp for a long time. I didn't know which way this was going to go. My guess was Marcus would decide to hide his sister in Beauchamp's basement. That's what I would tell Marcus to do, but I kept my mouth shut. I said nothing because when Beauchamp put his hands in his pockets, reflexively, I put my right hand in the pocket of my shorts. I felt the outline of the bus ticket my Poppy had given me early this morning and I realized I had a way out of this mess. Just grab my suitcase and run down Cranston Street and around the corner and jump on the first Greyhound bus headed north toward West Beaumont and safety. None of the insanity of Providence and Marcus and Beauchamp and Evelyn and Pele and Raja could touch me once I got on that bus. Just get on the bus. Leave it all behind and never think about it again back in West Beaumont where no one ever had to worry about the things Marcus and Sherri had to worry about. Finally, something simple.

"Stick that up your white ass."

Marcus and Leon and Henry and Ray turned and walked off in the direction Meme and Sherri took after Evelyn's murder. Just as abruptly, Beauchamp took his hands out of his pockets and walked up the stairs of his duplex and sat once again on his rocking chair. He took out a tin of tobacco and thrust a plug into his mouth. I watched him work it with his jaw until he puckered up and let fly a long streak of tobacco juice that sailed out onto the sidewalk where Evelyn had died not long ago. The juice splattered against Cranston Street and skipped in the direction of a bus carrying black people to wherever they were going. I stood there with my hand in my pocket and grasped the bus ticket and, instinctively, made my decision. I ran up the stairs of Meme and Poppy's duplex. I moved along the porch that was still covered in the wood fragments from the bullets that might have killed me if Sherri hadn't jumped on top of me. I opened the door and walked inside and moved toward the tiny bedroom that Poppy had already cleared of the shards of glass. I could see bullet holes in the drywall just over the bed I had slept on that morning.

I opened the closet where my tiny suitcase sat. I took my clothes from my drawer and stuffed them in the suitcase. I took my red, white, and blue ABA Julius Irving basketball and my gym bag and set them in Poppy's living room. I went to his bathroom and relieved myself and washed my hands. I grabbed the dirty towel that hung from the brass ring bolted into the bathroom wall. When I dried off my hands, the towel was even more dirty and grimy from when I used it to shower, just as I expected it to be. I came out of the bathroom and stepped around Poppy who carried wood and nails and a hammer so he could fix the sash of the bullet-ridden bedroom. He didn't say anything as he walked into the tiny bedroom and began prying off the busted wood and began replacing it with a new sash. I felt the gulf between us as he tried to fix that which was broken at the same time I was going to flee.

I bent over to pick up my suitcase and gym bag and ABA basketball and turned to open the door leading out onto the porch and down the steps and over Cranston Street to the Greyhound bus station less than a mile away. I opened the door to leave. Meme stood in the doorway. She had returned from getting Sherri back to her duplex. I could see her lips pulled tight against her face. I imagined it must have been terrible for my Meme to walk Sherri home after Evelyn's slaughter, and still, with all the pain and devastation Sherri and Marcus and Leon, and Henry, and Ray, my grandparents and Beauchamp, even Pele, with all they were going through, I was still running away.

"You're leaving?"

"You and Poppy said I am out, and after this," I gestured to the bedroom window where Poppy had replaced the old glass with a new one and the remaining dry wall with the stitching of bullet holes.

"No, Timothy, things are not the same. You have to stay."

"No, I'm out. They're trying to kill me, Meme. Raja saw me when he did the drive by and killed Evelyn." I waved the bus ticket Meme and Poppy gave me that morning. "You can live this way if you want. I still don't understand why you do, and after this, I really think you're stupid to stay. No, Meme, I'm out."

I stepped around her, bumping her slightly, and without looking back, I walked across the bullet-riddled porch and down the steps. I took a quick left, stepping around the blood-stained broken concrete where Evelyn had been gunned down. I put my head down when I walked in front of Beauchamp sitting in his rocking chair, his eyes glued to me and probably seeing me for what I really was. He said nothing as I walked down the street, but I could feel his stare piercing the back of my head, and then the feeling was gone, his eyes turning away from me as if he no longer thought me worthy of his consideration. I looked across the street to my right and saw basketball games going on and people sitting on the benches of the picnic tables and a police car cruising off in the distance and some black homeless person passed out in a gutter.

Cranston Street smelled of urine and barbeque and weed and cigarettes and sweat and car exhaust and molded rubber from the factory down the street, and diesel from the National Guard trucks at the armory, and cheeseburgers and cheap wine and body odor and flowers from a flower box that hung out from a tenement window. I heard babies crying and a bus grinding into gear and a police siren and the thump of a machine from the rubber factory, and laughing and gun shots and the thump of dominoes, and deep breathing and coughing and crying and doors opening and closing, and clothes being pulled off of clotheslines and arguments beginning and ending, and the slap of ropes from double-dutch.

I felt sweat soak through my shirt and the concentration of the heat of the street though my sneakers, and the thickness of the ozone that draped over Providence. My senses were overwhelmed, much like they had been since my dad dropped me off and it was all together too much, and I had had enough, and the bus station loomed up in front of me as I turned left and headed away from Cranston Street. The station had people moving in and out of the terminal and gleaming silver buses and yellow taxis, and people dropping off people from their cars and I felt like I walked in cement because I couldn't get there fast enough. I just needed to march in and see the person in the glass ticket booth and show him my ticket and get on the bus and leave this little portion of hell.

I heard thunderous music from down by the Armory. It grew in force as the bass beat boomed. I put my cheap suitcase down but continued to hold on to my gym bag and my ABA basketball. I turned back toward Cranston Street and through the wafting of heat, I could make out a dark car moving past the armory about a quarter mile away. The muscles in my arms began to bunch up and I could feel the tiny hairs on the back of my neck stand rigid. This was the same dark, menacing car that Raja's people drove when they gunned down Evelyn. I realized the dark car was moving toward me just fast enough that it would get to me before I could run into the bus station.

There was plenty of traffic and other people on the streets, so it was quite possible that Raja and his people had not seen me yet. I tried to move, but paralysis had taken over my body and I was stuck on the searing cement. It took too long, but eventually I broke out of my stupor. I looked across the street and saw old, wooden fencing that surrounded dilapidated tenements. I could make a dash for it and try to run into the bus station, or I could race across the street and jump the fence until Raja drove by, hoping he wouldn't see me. It was taking me too long to move. Raja's car drove through the intersection of Cranston Street and the boulevard where the bus station was located. I made my decision and grabbed my suitcase and sprinted across the street. I tried to throw my suitcase and basketball and gym bag over the fence. My suitcase and the basketball made it over, but the gym bag caught the edge of the fencing and bounced back toward me. Retrieving my gym bag added costly time, but I had to get it. It was precious to me. I reached the fencing and grabbed the handle of the old bag. I needed speed if I wanted to vault over the fence, so I moved back quickly and glancing back over my left shoulder, seeing Raja's car bearing down on me, I ran full speed and in one motion, bounded up the side of the fence, throwing my gym bag over at the same time.

My right knee caught the edge of the fence and I flipped over the top and somersaulted into the back yard of one of the run-down buildings. I landed full on my back and felt the air escape from my lungs. The boom of Raja's car had now drawn even to where I had leaped over the fence. I felt the rumble of the music from his car. It was loud enough to make the ground tremble under where I was lying. I heard doors open and slam shut. I grabbed my stuff and rolled backwards as close to the edge of the fencing as possible. The way I had rolled into the base of the fence allowed me to look straight up the ten feet to the top of the fence. In a few seconds, I could hear the sound of someone jumping up the other side. Two hands appeared at the top and a dark face peered over. I could see the dullness of the eyes of this man. I didn't know if it was Raja or just one of his gang. He hauled himself up so his waist balanced on the edge of the fencing. I could see him turn his head this way and that. Evidently, he was looking into the back of the tenements. Curiously, he did not look straight down because if he did, he would see me laying prone, cowering at the very base of the fencing. But he didn't. The music had been turned down in Raja's car and I heard the guy at the top of the fence yell.

"He gone. Don't see him nowhere."

"Get back in. We'll find him."

This second voice had to be Raja. It was full of menace. I tried to shimmy closer to the fence without making any noise. That's when I realized my gym bag was a few feet away from me and possibly in view of the guy at the top of the fence. If I reached out, my movement would alert the guy at the top of the fence and that would be it. If I let the bag sit there, the guy on the top of the fence might notice it. It was hidden in the shadows from the tenement not thirty feet from where I lay. At that moment, the setting sun broke between alleys that separated one tenement from another. It fully illuminated me and my gym bag, but apparently blinded the guy on the top of the fence. I watched him slide back over the side. His fingers let go of their grip and I heard the muffled sound of a man dropping back to the ground. First one door slammed shut and then another. Raja's car roared back to life. The music thundered out from inside the car. I felt the car roll away down the boulevard. I was still in full paralysis and I lay there until there was no evidence of the noises from Raja's car.

I reached over and grabbed the handles of my gym bag and pulled it close so that both of my arms wrapped around it, like a mother grasps on to her child in the middle of a storm. I lay that way until the sun slid beyond the alleys of the tenements and left me hidden at the base of the fencing. It was only then that I noticed I was not breathing. The air surged out from my lungs and I panted, desperately trying to force air into my lungs and into my brain so I could think of what I was going to do next. I felt safe smooshed up against the fencing, but I knew I couldn't stay there, and I couldn't jump over the fence. Raja's car could be parked nearby, and I would just be saying, "Kill me now." I tried to figure out where I was in relation to Cranston Street and Meme and Poppy's duplex. I realized that I was in the row of tenements that were situated behind Meme and Poppy's place. I figured if I could move between the buildings, I could work my way back. But I was still terrified and for the moment, I wasn't going anywhere.

Once again, it was another early evening in Providence where the heat was overpowering. I felt myself become drowsy and my eyelids begin to droop. My suitcase lay next to me along with my basketball. I continued to clutch my gym bag to my chest. Slowly, the shadows from the tenements reached out to me. I felt the slightest of breezes move through the alleys and the combination of shade and breeze cooled me for the first time since I arrived a few days ago.

I fell asleep and dreamed of being in my bed back in West Beaumont where I could slide open my bedroom window and hop down onto my back porch and take off my clothes and skinny-dip in my dad and my above-ground pool. I could feel the cool of the water envelop me. I could swim down to the bottom of the pool and feel the balance of pressure from inside my body and the weight of the water. I could open my eyes and look up through the darkness and see stars and the moon and the safety and the calm of the serene water. Then I could feel the hands of people wrenching me back up to the surface. I was naked to the world. In my dream, black people came and slapped at me and kicked me and spit on me until I woke with a scream, still curled up against the wooden fencing. It was pitch black and cars drove by on the other side of the fencing and people talked loudly and bottles broke not too far away. I shook my head to get rid of the remnants of the dream, but much of it remained etched in my mind and I could not shake it away for what seemed like a very long time.

# Chapter 18

## Raja

I began to calm down but realized that the dream wasn't far from the reality of it all. I let myself lay there and recover from the terror. Finally controlling my breathing, I knew I had to move and get to Meme and Poppy's duplex if I wanted to survive the night. I grabbed my suitcase and continued to clutch my gym bag. I decided to leave my basketball behind because I knew I couldn't carry everything, and it would be too cumbersome to try. I stood up and took the ball and wedged it firmly into the corner of where two fences met behind the tenements. I saw some old, dirty newspapers that were stained with some filth. They weren't far away. I crawled on my belly to keep out of sight and grabbed them and crawled back and tried to conceal the basketball as best I could. I had to leave it behind if I wanted to get to where I needed to go. I moved off, cloaked in shadow.

First, I rushed to where there was linen hanging from clothes lines. I squatted down in the dark and listened. I could not hear any cars nearby, but I could hear people talking in the alley. Their muffled conversations were punctuated by spits of fire from whatever they were smoking. I slid through the linen and saw a dumpster that sat behind the next tenement. I scurried low until I slid behind the dumpster. It stank of old eggs and fish and potatoes and molded bread. As I sat, I could feel damp under my backside and where my hands kept me balanced. It was the same smell as the smell near Marcus' tenement: human urine and feces. I grabbed my gym bag so it wouldn't get soiled and popped back up. The stench made me retch. I stood there puking for a few minutes until I thought there was nothing left to puke. I dry-heaved for the next minute or so until I was dizzy. The smell of urine and human waste wasn't going away. Gathering my strength in spite of my nausea, I darted, half bent over, toward the darkness of the next tenement.

I ran along and suddenly, I slammed into a wooden fence that I could not see in the blackness. I was knocked backwards and I let out a yell that I was sure someone would hear. I couldn't hear anyone moving toward me, so I lay there in the darkness until I could gather myself. My eyes adjusted and I could see the wooden fence was a little shorter in height than the fence I jumped when I escaped from Raja. Once again, I threw my stuff over the fence. This time, I moved back a bit farther and sprinted forward. I leaped and hurdled the fence like track stars did on my dad's high school track team. I ripped my trail leg over the fence and landed on the foot of my lead leg. I carried my sprint until I could get it under control. Still, there were no sounds that might suggest anyone was near. Whatever the black people were doing tonight, they were doing it in front of their tenements and not behind them.

I pulled myself over close to the fence again. I estimated that my Poppy and Meme's duplex had to be close. I stood back up and through the darkness, I could make out a single light coming from the back porch of either my grandparent's duplex or Beauchamp's, but I was still disoriented enough not to know which one. Either way, I needed to slip through the next alley and I would be in the safety of their backyard. I took my suitcase and gym bag and moved quietly through the alley. Then I heard something that froze me. It was the voices of men walking down Cranston Street. My first thought was it was Raja, but as the men drew closer, I recognized the voice of Pele. He and his men had to be level with Beauchamp's duplex. Through a lone street light, I could make out Pele, still wearing his all-black outfit and black hat with the big "P" on the front. I slipped closer, pretty sure that I was invisible in the black of the alley.

They couldn't be more than fifty feet away as I was now in Beauchamp's alley leading to his backyard. I could see that Pele, along with the rest of his gang, had what looked like bulges in the back of their pants. As they moved past Beauchamp's, I could see a gleam from the street lights. Pele and his buddies were armed.

I guess that didn't surprise me much. They kept moving and after a bit, I could no longer hear them talking. I sunk down on my backside behind Beauchamp's duplex and tried to peer through the darkness.

Beauchamp's backyard was small, just like my grandparent's backyard. He had built a chain link fence to separate his backyard from my grandparent's. At that moment, I heard a rattling coming from the fence. First, one figure then another hauled themselves up and over Beauchamp's fence and dropped lightly to the ground. Their movements were precise and measured and athletic. They moved as shadows toward Beauchamp's back porch. One of them remained hidden behind the porch while the next one stole quietly up the wooden steps. Now I could see the figure clearly. It was a man with a bright red bandana that held his afro in place who stepped into the faint light. It was Marcus. He gently knocked on the back door of Beauchamp's duplex. In a few moments, the door slid open, perhaps maybe a foot, and I could see Beauchamp's mug clearly. He and Marcus spoke quietly. Marcus began to gesture emphatically with his hands and Beauchamp crossed his arms across his chest. Marcus put out one hand and placed it on Beauchamp's shoulder. There was another pause. Marcus turned and spoke into the darkness. The hidden figure moved up the staircase. It was Sherri. She was wearing mostly black, so it was hard to make her out, but as soon as she moved closer to Beauchamp, he dropped his arms from across his chest and stepped aside, letting Marcus and Sherri enter.

I hadn't realized I wasn't breathing until I heard the loud noise of air escaping from my lungs. I tried to control my breathing, thinking I was disturbing the silence. Even in Providence and in this dire situation, I was self-absorbed, like my mere breathing would upset the stillness and cause a disturbance. Either way, I felt a sense of relief knowing that Sherri was still alive, even with Raja prowling about. I decided I was going to knock on Beauchamp's door too. Beauchamp had allowed me to see a different feature of his personality, one that maybe no one else on

Cranston Street had seen. Even though he was revolting and probably hated by the black families around where he lived, there must have been some sort of trust of him or else Marcus would not have tried to sneak Sherri over. Marcus must have understood, perhaps deep within himself, that if Sherri was going to stay alive, she was going to need Beauchamp to keep her that way, white man or not.

I gathered up my suitcase and gym bag, but as I did so, my body stiffened. I could hear, off in the distance, a booming stereo from a car moving down Cranston Street, coming in the direction of my grandparent's and Beauchamp's duplex. The music gradually pulsed louder until it seemed to be only yards away. I really couldn't know from whose car the music blasted, but something told me Raja was driving in the same direction as he did yesterday when he gunned down Evelyn, making his first move toward driving Pele out. And then I remembered that Pele and his guys had just moved passed. Nothing good was going to come of this.

I crouched as low as I could. When I was as low and close to Beauchamp's wall as possible, a hail of gunfire erupted right in front of Beauchamp's duplex. I could make out the dark, familiar silhouette of Raja's car, windows open, flashes from guns hammering. I heard screams and returning gunfire. A shotgun blast boomed above the sounds of the other guns. Bullets whizzed above my head and shattered the metal fencing that Marcus and Sherri had just scrambled over moments before. I couldn't take my eyes away from the gap in the alley as the war raged. As the tumult of the gunfire reached its apex, three dark figures sprinted around the front of Beauchamp's duplex, firing over their shoulders as they ran. One of them stopped to take better aim at Raja's car. He got off two or three quick, whack, whack, whack shots before his body spun around and he fell face first onto the dilapidated tar of the alley. He rolled onto his stomach and then tried to get up on his knees. He crawled forward for a few yards, and then he fell again and this time remained motionless. His two buddies kept running and shooting and ran right past where I remained hidden, pressed up against the edge of Beauchamp's duplex. They leaped up the fencing and vaulted over, disappearing into the dark as gunfire continued to fly around them.

I looked back and saw Raja's car. The back window had been blown out. One final, ear-piercing shot rang out. The driver of Raja's car must have been hit, because the car careened out of control and spun sideways, slamming headlong into a telephone pole. The front passenger door was flung open. A dark figure ran around and grabbed a figure that was slumped down over the steering wheel. The man hauled the body out and flung it onto the sidewalk like a ragdoll. He jumped back into the driver's seat, closed the door, and backed away from the telephone pole. The front of the car was crumpled, with smoke and steam rising fitfully from the engine. As he backed away, another bullet whizzed over the hood of the car and slammed into the telephone pole. Dark pieces of wood flew.

The car continued to back away, running over the dead man who had been tossed out of the car. The guy driving hit the gas. It wheezed and coughed like a dying animal. As its tires spun, the body of the dead man under the car was caught in the wheel wells. I heard the snapping of bones and ripping of flesh until finally, the car dislodged itself from the human speed bump. I heard the engine scream away, and then in the distance, tires squealed as the driver shifted from first gear into second, until finally the noise of the car faded and a unnerving calm settled in. I was frozen in place as a deathly quiet hung over Cranston Street. Two more dark shapes appeared at the end of Beauchamp's alley. One of them bent down and checked on the guy who lay dead. He put his hand on the dead guy's forehead, like a parent would do if a child had a fever. He squatted that way for a few more seconds while his friend stood near. Finally, he got up and began to walk down the alley in my direction. There was a steady clap of boots moving in my direction. I tried to flatten myself even more as he approached.

When he was even with me, he stopped and turned to look at me in the darkness. I don't know how he could have spied me as I clung to the side of Beauchamp's duplex. He was dressed all in black. He wore a black baseball cap with a "P" that reflected the only light that shone dimly from one of the tenements. He wore sunglasses. He stood there in the darkness and then raised his arm and pointed a gun at me. The barrel couldn't have been more than six inches from my eyes. He stood there in the dark and I could see his eyes as his sunglasses slid slightly down his nose. They looked lifeless and devoid of compassion, but as he continued to point his gun at my forehead, I could make out a tiny glimmer. Just for a moment, his eyes exposed grief. It didn't last, but it was there nonetheless. I saw it in his eyes, and he saw that I saw it. He took his other hand and slid the sunglasses back up the bridge of his nose.

I slid up from my cowering position and stood up in the darkness. Wet began to form at my crotch. I could smell the stink of my own urine as it flowed down my pant leg. I realized I was about to be killed just yards from where my grandparents lived. I would be just another dead boy added to the long list of people who died in Providence that night. I began to raise my hands in front of my face to beg not to be killed when slowly, the man lowered his gun. The surprise of it shocked me, and I felt my bowels give out and I soiled myself. The combination of seeing people killed and the memory of Evelyn's blood and just me being in a place where I did not belong loosened my intestines. It was too much, and I began to weep like a little kid whose friends abandoned him at the playground.

The man with the sunglasses and black baseball cap with the "P" and his friend walked away. They simply walked off and turned right and disappeared into the projects. I fell to the ground in my own puddle of piss, my shorts heavy with soil. I lay that way in my filth for what seemed like an eternity until finally, I pulled myself up and crawled on my hands and knees and reached out and felt the staircase leading up to Beauchamp's duplex. I continued to crawl one stair at a time until I reached Beauchamp's stoop. I reached up with one hand and knocked on the door while my other hand covered the growing stains on my pants. In a moment, it opened. Beauchamp stood there, peering into the darkness. It took him a moment to look down and see me lying prone on his stoop. He looked down at me for a moment and then, without speaking, he reached down and lifted me up, holding me in his arms like a child. His strength was startling, considering his age and outward look of being so unhealthy. He put his foot onto the bottom of his back door and pushed it open. He moved silently and still cradling me in his arms, he closed the door behind him with his other foot.

I was in his kitchen. He set me down on the floor carefully and moved off. As he left his kitchen, he picked up a hand gun that sat on his counter. He crouched down and moved into his living room. I took a deep breath and inhaled my stench. It was only then that I noticed two other figures lying on the floor underneath Beauchamp's kitchen table. My eyes began to focus in the darkness, and I saw Marcus and Sherri. They lay on the floor, huddled together. They said nothing to me as I lay there. I looked up and saw that the archway between Beauchamp's kitchen and living room was riddled with bullet holes. Splinters of wood chips lay on the polished hard-wood floor. I knew I stunk and there was no way for me to hide it. I curled up in a ball of humiliation. Still, Marcus and Sherri said nothing. What should they say? How does someone react to gunfire and murder and a disgusting white kid curled up on the floor?

Beauchamp came back in. He stood this time instead of crouching. He reached up and pulled down on a string that hung from a ceiling light. My eyes squinted as the light flooded the kitchen. Beauchamp had a roll of clothing in his arm. He looked at me and reached out with his three-fingered hand.

"Take these. There's a shower over there."

He pointed to a door. I stood up, soaked and stinking. I took the clothes from Beauchamp, and bending over, tried to hide the stains that I knew everyone could see. I moved quickly to the door and opened it. It was a tiny bathroom with an impossibly small shower tucked into a corner. I quickly took off my sweat-soaked t-shirt. I fumbled to remove my gym shorts. My hands had to pass through the piss and soil. I couldn't help but get some of it on me. I took my ruined shorts and threw them in the toilet to let the crap seep out. I turned on the shower and didn't bother to adjust the temperature. I wanted the piss and soil off of me and I didn't care if the water was frigid, which it was.

The water coursed over me and I used my hands to frantically wipe off the feces that stuck to my crotch and thighs. Most of it washed off into the bottom of the shower. A swirl of brown drained away and finally I could relax. There was no shampoo in the shower; just a thick bar of coarse soap. I stepped away from the stream of water and grabbed the soap and began to scrub the grime and the sweat and the disgust off of my body. I ran the soap through my hair and did my best to scrub it clean. My body was covered in white soap suds. I stood there looking down at myself. Finally, I stepped back into the stream and washed off the suds and used my hands to keep scrubbing at my skin. No matter how much I scrubbed, I didn't think I was cleaning my body of the filth.

I turned off the cold water and reached out for the towel that hung from a rack. I used it to dry off, but mostly, I used it to exfoliate every part of my body, like whatever skin I had needed to be scrubbed away completely before I stepped out of the shower. When I was done, my body was pink from the scouring. When I felt that maybe I was clean enough and dry enough, I dropped the wet towel down on the floor of the shower and stepped out. I was naked and Beauchamp's duplex remained silent. I reached over, and grabbing the roll of clothes, I put on a faded olive-colored shirt that said "Marines" and put my legs through a pair of white boxer shorts. I grabbed the pair of pants. They were clean, even though I could see the remnant stains of many streams of tobacco juice running up and down each pant leg. I zipped up the zipper of the pants and pushed the waist button through the hole. I noticed there was a small window in the bathroom. I peered outside and saw Beauchamp, gun still in his hand, walk quickly up his back porch steps. He held my suitcase and my gym bag and quickly looked around him to make sure he was not seen. I jumped back quickly from the window so he wouldn't see that I was looking out at him.

I picked up the wet towel and draped it over the top of the shower. I reached into the toilet where my soiled clothes floated. I reached back into the shower and grabbed the bar of soap. I put it on the edge of the toilet seat and used my bare hands to twist out the remaining piss and crap. When I felt most of it had been squeezed out, I picked up my clothes, and still holding them over the toilet bowl, flushed the piss and remaining soil down the toilet. I repeated the operation three or four more times. Finally, I grabbed the soap and began to wash the clothes. I knew they would never come clean, but I kept at it until at least they looked better. I thrust the clothes in and out of the toilet water. I flushed the toilet, keeping my clothes in the swirl of water to wash out the soap. When I thought they were rinsed clean as best they could be, I took my clothes and wrung them out four or five times. I carefully carried the t-shirt and shorts and underwear from the toilet to the shower and hung them on the curtain rod. I was able to do this without leaking any more water on Beauchamp's floor.

I took a deep breath and opened the door that led out to the kitchen. Beauchamp and Marcus and Sherri stood there waiting. They seemed agitated that I had taken so long. Just then, we all turned our heads. We heard the sound of multiple police car sirens barreling toward us from the other end of Cranston Street. Beauchamp moved quickly and bending over, used his fingernails to pry up a hidden board in his kitchen floor. He pulled it back and exposed a bronze handle. With an effortless motion, he pulled up on the handle and more boards moved out of the way. I could see a ladder that led down into darkness.

"The police are here. They can't find you. Get down the ladder."

Beauchamp took Sherri's hand and guided her to the top steps of the ladder.

"There's a light switch on the wall when you reach the bottom. Down you go."

He let go of her hand and she began her descent. Marcus stepped down right behind her.

"You too. I don't want the police finding you either. People talk in Providence. The police might be wondering why a kid from the suburbs has been around when black kids were getting killed. Get down there."

He took me by the shoulder and guided me toward the hole in his floor. I took two steps down the ladder and stopped and looked up at Beauchamp. I was wearing his clothes, the same guy I despised just a few days ago, and now he thought I should be hiding from the police and I wasn't arguing. He looked at me and nodded his head like he was saying, "Go down. It will be ok." He smiled. It exposed his green-stained teeth. They didn't seem so disgusting to me anymore. Actually, as he smiled, his eyes shone in the light of his kitchen. For the first time, I really looked into his eyes. There was kindness in them. He had been through a tough life of his own, and now he was helping out the people he hated, or at least gave the impression that he hated. I smiled back and lowered myself into the basement where Marcus and Sherri waited.

# Chapter 19

## Plans in the Dark

The light was on, and as I took the last step into the basement, I could hear the floor boards slide back and the trap door shut. I heard Beauchamp's footsteps move across his kitchen floor toward his living room.

The three of us stood silently. I could hear the faintest ringing of a doorbell and muffled voices that I thought had to be the police talking with Beauchamp. Marcus took my arm and took Sherri's arm and moved us into the corner of the basement. He pulled us to the floor, and we sat crisscross applesauce and tried to keep our breathing from making any kind of sound. From where I sat, I could hear Beauchamp and the police clearly.

"There's a dead colored in your alley and another one in front of your house."

"I didn't know that."

"What did you see?"

"It's more what I heard."

"Tell us."

"I was sitting on my rocking chair in my living room, watching the Red Sox on TV. I heard some boys talking as they walked by the front of my house. I didn't get up to see who it was. I heard a car engine roar from the end of Cranston Street. Then I heard pop, pop, pop, like firecrackers going off. We hear that a lot around here, but those sounds were close, so I jumped on the floor and stayed there. That's when bullets sprayed my house. I heard some screams and more shots. It was quiet for a second and then I heard a loud boom, like a shotgun blast. I heard tires squeal and then a crash. I could hear car doors open and then slam shut and a car gun its engine and drive off. I never left my floor. It was quiet after that and I didn't hear anything else. I was too busy hugging the floor."

"Did you get up to see what happened outside?"

"Yes."

"Well? Tell us what the hell you saw."

"I told you, I didn't see anything."

"You didn't see the nigger in your alley or the dead one on Cranston Street in front of your house?"

"Never looked to see anything outside. I was worried about my house. The coloreds shot it up pretty good while they were trying to kill each other."

"Do you mind if we look around?"

"Be careful of the broken glass."

"Stay here. We might have more questions."

I heard footsteps moving through Beauchamp's home. At first, the footsteps seemed to move toward the front of his duplex. I heard some muffled voices, but then the footsteps moved directly over us and then toward Beauchamp's kitchen. They stopped pretty close to where the floorboards were that hid Beauchamp's entry to his hidden basement. Sherri grabbed onto Marcus' hand and pulled him close. Stupidly, we had left the light switch on. Maybe some of the light could leak though the floorboards. I got up and moved quickly to the light switch. I quietly turned it off, trying not to make any clicking sound with the switch. I scurried back to where Marcus and Sherri sat on the floor. This time, I sat close to Sherri. She reached out her hand and took mine and squeezed it so hard I thought she might break my fingers. I didn't pull away, because frankly, I needed the comfort. I felt like I might piss myself again.

Above us, we could hear the floor creak in the kitchen and then move back over our heads and toward Beauchamp's living room. I heard more sirens and car doors opening and closing.

"If you think of anything or see anything, call us. Here's my card."

Beauchamp didn't say a word. I could hear the front door open and close and footsteps echo off of Beauchamp's front porch. I'm sure things were still going on outside. Maybe they were taking the dead bodies away. I didn't know. How would I know about anything that happened to the people of Providence? I was in a TV show; at least it was surreal enough to be one. *White kid visits grandparents and gets involved in gang warfare.* I didn't think anyone could make this stuff up, but there I was.

The three of us sat in the darkened basement for what seemed like hours. I said nothing and Marcus and Sherri said nothing, and we waited. My backside began to ache, and I shifted my position. Doing so broke the hand hold Sherri and I had maintained the entire time. We heard footsteps again moving from the living room to the kitchen. I heard a grating sound as the floorboards were removed and the opening that led down to the basement revealed a single beam of light from Beauchamp's kitchen. First one foot and then another descended the ladder. It was Beauchamp. He turned on the light. I was blind for a bit, but my eyes eventually adjusted.

Now that I had time and the danger seemed to have left us, I could see that Beauchamp's basement was much bigger than I thought. It had wood paneling from one side to the next. The floors were polished just like upstairs. Two couches sat facing one another and there was another easy chair not far from the ladder leading upstairs. The couches and the easy chair matched perfectly. A small radio sat on a table next to the easy chair. Coasters for drinks were placed around the room on different tables. Beauchamp had a small bar that was situated at the far end of the basement. There were four barstools with leather seats and high backs. I wondered who Beauchamp had for friends that he would need four barstools, and then I thought about his wife and how she made their duplex their home. Beauchamp must have wanted it to stay the way she had decorated it before she died. I looked around some more and noticed there were no windows at all. No one could see in and I couldn't see out. Again, another surprise from Beauchamp.

"The police are gone. They hauled the bodies away but stayed awhile, using their flashlights to check out my backyard. There was nothing back there. Police don't stay around to really check things out when the coloreds kill each other. That's just the way it is."

He eyed me when he said this, and I remembered how he had retrieved my suitcase and gym bag from where I hid when the bullets flew.

"They told me I needed a new porch because of all the bullets weakening the frame. The last thing they said was I should get the hell out of Providence. It was no place for white people. One of the cops was white. The other one was black. The white cop did all the talking. The black cop just stared at me like he knew something but couldn't say anything."

Beauchamp motioned for us to get off the floor and sit on a couch. We got up and I moved to sit next to Sherri and Marcus. Marcus kind of nudged me like "Don't sit with us" so I sat in the opposite facing couch.

"Didn't want your help. Raja kept driving by where I live. Leon said I should bring Sherri here while it was dark. He told me to sneak through the projects and jump your fence. I didn't want it. The last time Raja drove by though, he stop right in front of our house. My mother was home, and she walked outside and stared at Raja. He drove off, but by then I realized Leon was right. I had to get Sherri here. Still don't like that I need help from you."

Marcus' eyes squinted and his forehead furrowed, making his afro kind of bob up and down.

"It will be just tonight. Evelyn's funeral going to be tomorrow. Her daddy and mommy want it quick. You still going?" Marcus turned to Sherri and she made that same motion where she cocked her head and lifted her eyebrow as if to say, "Damn right I'm going." Anyway, we out tomorrow."

"What do you plan to do then?"

"Don't know yet."

Marcus looked at his sister. She looked down her long legs to her skinny ankles and nodded. I had no idea how any of us were going to survive this. Maybe I could stay and help, or maybe I could make another dash for the bus station in the morning; risk Raja's people seeing me. Raja knew I hadn't left, so whatever he planned on doing to Sherri, he probably still planned on doing to me. I was stuck in this black world and I hated it. And from the way I understood it, I needed black people to help me out. It didn't make me much different from Marcus in that way. Maybe that was the only way we were really alike. It wasn't jump shots or fancy dribbling or power dunks. It was me being totally helpless and foreign and alone and outnumbered, needing black people I hardly knew to bail me out, just like Marcus and Sherri needed Beauchamp. I detested the idea. I had just wanted to play hoop with the brothers. I felt the resentment bubble up and I hated feeling that way and hated that I had to feel that way.

"What might you do?"

Beauchamp went around the bar and pulled four Narragansett beers out from a refrigerator hidden under the countertop. We heard the unmistakable whump that refrigerator doors make when they close and hermetically seal whatever is inside. He walked over to us, and using his hands, twisted off the caps and handed each one of us a bottle. Marcus' face kind of bunched up in surprise when he saw that one of Beauchamp's hands had only three fingers and some of the meat of his hand was missing. Marcus took the bottle anyway. I had never drunk beer before. Marcus took a long swig from his bottle. Sherri took a sip. Beauchamp looked at Marcus and Sherri and then me as he held the bottle to his lips and drained the entire thing. I tilted the bottle back and took a long pull, immediately coughing when I took the bottle from my lips. Marcus and Sherri just looked at me. Beauchamp gave a bit of a "huh" when I had finished coughing, like he knew that I wasn't a drinker. I was beginning to think Beauchamp knew a great deal about me, even from just the few days I had been in Providence. I didn't like that feeling either.

"Pele says we need to kill Raja. He says if we don't kill him, Raja definitely will kill us. No way out of it."

I looked at Marcus and Sherri saw me staring at him.

"I don't like him being involved."

Sherri made a slight nod in my direction.

"You should have thought about that when you decided to hang out with him on the porch when Evelyn got killed."

"He's done nothing to deserve this. He just picked the wrong week to be on Cranston Street."

"And you don't think he be part of why Raja after us?"

"I don't."

"Maybe he not the reason, but he done complicate things for Raja."

"Tell me about your plan, Marcus."

Beauchamp stood up from his easy chair and got himself another two beers, handing one to Marcus and keeping one for himself. Once again, he drained it all. This time so did Marcus.

"Sherri going to the funeral. Everyone going, my mom, Leon's dad and mom, Ray's mom, Henry's grandparents." He looked at me. "Your grandparents." I hadn't even thought about Meme and Poppy, that's how much of a prick I had been. Beauchamp saw me recoil at the mention of my grandparents.

"Don't worry. They're OK. The bullets only hit my house, this time."

Marcus took another deep breath.

"Evelyn's mom and dad. They broken. The rest of Cranston Street and just 'bout everyone on it. Evelyn was good. She didn't deserve it. None of us do."

He paused for a bit and then looked right at me.

"We using you."

No one moved. I felt like I might soil myself again and my stomach churned like I was about to puke.

"What do you mean you're using me?"

"Pele's idea. His people are going to be mixing in at the funeral. You come in to pay your respects. Pele know Raja going to be close. We wait until Raja make a move. Then we kill him, and it be over."

Beauchamp held the beer in his hand and looked at me, maybe thinking I would bolt up the stairs and run to the bus station right then. I could. I still had the ticket in my pocket. Maybe Marcus understood what I was thinking.

"You'd never make it. Raja's people everywhere and they looking to kill any of Pele's people on sight and they certainly be looking for a white boy. The only way is to take Raja out at the funeral. Remember, you a insect to Pele. If you die, it's nothing to him. He doing this for business. And maybe for Sherri and Evelyn. Pele is rotting, but a piece of him is still his own. If he thinks he can take out Raja and keep his business and keep my sister alive, that what he do. The best way is for you to pull Raja and his people out of the shadows at the funeral so we can kill him."

"Who knows about this?" Beauchamp walked over and sat on the couch with me.

"Pele and his boys. Leon, Henry, Ray, me, Sherri."

"Your mom?"

"No. She don't know nothing 'bout the plan."

"You going to have a gun, Marcus?"

"I am."

"That will change everything for you, Marcus. You'll never come back from that."

Marcus sat on the couch for a moment before he spoke.

"That being white, what you saying. I thank you, Beauchamp, for taking my sister in and lying to the police about what you saw when the shooting start. But what you don't understand is no black man worry about coming back. It be just another day in the life of a poor nigger man on Cranston Street in Providence, Rhode Island. We stuck in this hell. They ain't no jobs. School no good. Housing is for shit. Nobody worrying about what black man or woman die. Not up on Capitol Hill where the mayor and good governor do worse things than anything we done. Matter of fact, Beauchamp, we think they want us to kill each other off. What's one more dead nigger to them?"

Beauchamp stood up from the couch and went back to the bar for his third beer. He came back around and looked at it a bit. The light in the basement reflected off the silver Narragansett label. I could make out my image on the label. So could all of us and so could Beauchamp. He looked at himself in the label for a while.

"You're right. What's one more dead nigger? It's been that way for a long time. No one will really care."

"You care, Beauchamp? Huh? You care about another dead nigger?"

"I do."

When he said this, I remembered all the times he spat at black people walking in front of his duplex and the awful things he said to them. I also remembered that what he showed to the people outside on Cranston Street wasn't all of him. I'd been inside his house and now I'm inside his basement and I felt safe. Beauchamp looked at Marcus intently for a few moments. He took a short, quick breath and spoke.

"I won't ever know what it is like to be a black man. Anyone say they don't see color is lying, and too many people in this country lie. So, you're right. No one will care if Raja is gone, or Pele, or any of you. You're just killing yourself off. That's why they have cities so they can lock you in and never let you out."

Beauchamp stood there in his basement and kind of looked up at the ceiling. Wherever he was at that moment wasn't here. He spoke like he was far away. His voice was low and had a slight tremble to it.

"I fought for my country and I fought with black men. We were all poor because poor people fight rich men's wars. Black poor, white poor, Hispanic poor, Indian poor. I saw black people blown to bits, guys I was eating with in a foxhole moments before. I saw that our country didn't give a shit about the poor people who didn't come back from Korea, or Vietnam, and certainly not the ones who did. That's what I see. I see the squalor and the filth and the desperation on Cranston Street. I look stupid to most people, but I could sell this place and get a loan and move out tomorrow; sell to some slum lord and buy a place down on the shore or over in Connecticut. I know black men from Cranston Street don't get loans. The banks making coin off the blacks in the tenements, so why make the change? I don't care about a black man getting gunned down in my alley. But I do care about another poor man getting gunned down." Beauchamp stood there for a few moments before he went on.

"When I can't take it, I come inside and listen to the game or climb down into my basement, because down here, I can't hear the gunshots and the stabbings and the wailing. I've seen too much."

Beauchamp stood rigid in the basement and I could see him squeezing his beer bottle. The muscles in his hands and forearms and biceps bulged under his shirt. We all sat there staring at him as he kept up the pressure until finally, the beer bottle burst, sending foam and glass flying in every direction. We didn't expect it and the explosion sent a shock wave through all of us.

Sherri clung to her brother like she might explode herself. Beer streamed down Beauchamp's hand and arm and down his pant leg. He stood in a puddle of foam mixed with shards of glass, and he did not move or react and maybe even notice what he had just done. Sherri got up and ran to the bar and grabbed a towel and got down on her knees to soak up the beer that surrounded Beauchamp's feet. She did that with one hand while carefully picking up the pieces of glass with her other hand. Beauchamp stood motionless for another few seconds and then snapped out of wherever it was that he had just been.

"I'm sorry. Let me help you with my mess."

"No, Beauchamp, I'll take care of your mess. Go sit down now." Beauchamp moved away from Sherri and sat down again on his easy chair. His bulk made it sag and there was a sigh that came from the springs deep inside.

"Where you go, just then, when you busted your beer bottle?" Marcus scooched up on the couch so he could sit up straight and rest his hands on his knees.

"Korea." Beauchamp said it softly, like no one could hear. "I go back to Korea. Every time one of you kills another, the booms and pops and cracks of guns can send me back to the time when other poor people like me were getting blown up or shot or stabbed. Sometimes it's worse than others. When I know I can't take it, I crawl down here and try to find some peace."

Beauchamp reached up to scratch his forehead where the scar shone fully. He used his three-fingered hand to do the scratching. Marcus looked at him for a while.

"So, move. You done said it yourself. Get out like the rest of you whiteys. Move down to Warwick or Kinston or Newport. Get the hell out."

"I won't. This is my wife's house and I'm not leaving it."

"Meme told me your wife was killed when she got hit by a car."

Sherri stood after she finished cleaning up and dropped the towel and glass shards into a waste basket. She sat down on the couch next to her brother.

"That's right. She got run over by a colored."

"She got run over by a poor person in Providence, you mean."

Beauchamp sat for a moment. A single tear formed just below his eye and slowly coursed down his face.

"Yes. A poor person."

"She could have been run over by any one. She was just at the wrong corner on the wrong street at a time when she shouldn't have been there. Like your friends in Korea who got blown up. They shouldn't have been there, either."

"You won't understand."

"And you say you can't understand what it's like to be black. Maybe we all should just start there and admit that none of us really knows what it's like to be anyone else but ourselves."

"Maybe."

He coughed and we all looked at the floor like we could find answers in his polished wood. Beauchamp looked over to Marcus.

"OK. I'll keep Sherri and Tim safe until the funeral. Sherri, I'll find some nice clothes you can wear so you don't have to go back to your house. That would be too dangerous. Tim, you might be able to fit into a suit I have. In the meantime, Marcus, what are you going to do?

"I have to meet my boys and make sure we set with the plan. Pele all set. They going to blend in at the funeral, but me and Henry and Ray and Leon, we have to be seen. You too, Sherri. You be with us. The church just a few blocks away, toward the bus station. Tim, you just walk out Beauchamp's front door and down Cranston Street and right to the church. Raja and his boys will be near, waiting for the right time to kill us and you. They won't realize we be waiting to kill them."

"Are you sure this is the way, Marcus?"

Sherri looked at her brother. He didn't smile or hold her hand or touch her at all.

"It's the only way."

He was done talking. He stood up quickly and stepped toward the ladder and climbed up. When he disappeared, we heard the back door to Beauchamp's duplex open and close quickly. Marcus was gone, doing I guess what he had to do.

# Chapter 20

## One on One

"I'll get some nice clothes for the both of you. You can try them on in the morning. Sleep down here on the couches. I'll be upstairs putting my house back together."

Beauchamp got off the couch and moved past where Sherri sat. He gently put his hand on her shoulder. Sherri put her hand on top of his and their hands held on for a while until finally, Beauchamp moved away, climbed the ladder, replaced the floorboards, and was gone. I waited a bit before all that was inside me bubbled up and burst out.

"What the hell?" I stood up from my couch and began to pace around the basement. I was involved in a plan to get rid of Raja and I had no say in it. "Why don't I just leave, and you people can take care of this on your own?" I reached into my pocket and pulled out the bus ticket. "It's not my problem. None of this is my problem."

"What about Meme and Poppy?"

"I'm not sure they're my problem either."

Sherri tipped the bottle of beer that was now warm in her hand up to her lips and took a very small sip. Her eyes never left mine as she removed the bottle from her mouth.

"You mean that?"

"They chose to stay here when they could have left a long time ago, so whatever happens on Cranston Street is of their choosing. They had to know things like this would happen with..."

"With what, the coloreds?"

"I didn't say that."

She looked at me some more and then dropped her chin so she

was looking at the floor.

"What do you think you know about us coloreds?"

I walked over to the bar and reached back into the refrigerator and pulled out another beer. I don't know why I did that since the beer Beauchamp had already given me was still mostly full. It took me quite a while before I said anything.

"You're just not what I expected."

"What did you expect? Do you think the things you want aren't the things we want?"

"Of course not."

"Then what is it? Do you think we should be living a better life and in a better place?"

"Maybe."

"And how do you think we should get that better life?"

"Want it more, I guess. Go to college. Get a good job. Move out. I don't know."

"So, you think we're in Providence because we don't want "it" more, whatever "it" is?"

"I have black friends back home who wanted it enough that they came to school in my hometown. I think they want something better for themselves."

"So, I should find a scholarship that sends me and my brother to West Beaumont so we can be happy like you?"

She put the emphasis on the "Beau" in Beaumont. It sounded crass when she pronounced it that way.

"Don't cut it down like that."

"But you can cut down Cranston Street?"

"I've never cut down Cranston Street."

"You never said it that way, but you had your preconceptions and found them to be inaccurate. That's cutting down Cranston Street. You didn't know the truth, or you think you knew the truth and when it slapped you in the face, you acted surprised or confused."

She stood up and sat next to me on the couch.

"Tim, how'd you get to West Beaumont?"

"I was born there."

"Exactly."

She pointed a finger at me when she said it and then sat back against the couch. I didn't know what she meant.

"My grandfather fought in World War II. He married my grandmother before he went off to load trucks for the white soldiers at the front. He got strafed by German planes and had a truck shot out from under him in Holland. Saved a few soldiers by racing back to rescue them when they got cut off from their unit. Got no medal for it. Just doing his job. He got home and tried to go to college, but the government wasn't loaning money to black soldiers. He lived in Providence not far from here. He worked his whole life, he and my grandmother, trying to save enough money to buy a house. Every time he thought he had saved up enough, someone moved the red line just far enough that no matter what money he had, they wouldn't take his down-payment or give him a loan. First, it was just the Cranston Street neighborhood that got red-lined, then most of Providence. He and my grandmother never had their chance, no matter how much they worked for it. Black people work hard, Tim."

I looked at her as she tried to help me understand poverty.

"All our families work. Ray's, Henry's, Leon's dad. My mom. We're not lazy. We're just trapped."

"I don't understand."

"Of course, you don't, Tim. Not many people worried about black men after the war. White folk got their loans and went to their colleges and bought their homes in West Beaumont or places like that and never thought twice about a system that was set up in their favor, even if many of those same people would have been disgusted by the truth of it."

Maybe a flicker of understanding seeped into my mind, but there were too many new truths for me to sort out, and I was still stuck on some of the early ones from this week. My brain had descended into a semi-permanent state of circuit overload. I couldn't process things fast enough, so most of the things I needed to understand were beyond my comprehension, at least at the time.

"How many affordable homes are there in West Beaumont, Tim?"

"Not many."

"Don't you think it strange? Do you think there might be a reason your town doesn't have housing like that? Who do you think would buy those houses, Tim?"

"Black families."

"That's right. People who want it more would move to West Beaumont, but your town has zoning laws. Modern day green lines and yellow lines, and red lines. Zoning laws just a fancy word for it."

Sherri kept pounding me with things I didn't want to know or things I didn't want to think about, all while we sat in Beauchamp's basement knowing someone was going to die tomorrow.

"You believe in God, Tim?"

"Most of the time."

"Do you think God decided to put you in West Beaumont and decided to put me in Providence?"

I didn't know what to think about that.

"Do you think God chooses our parents and where we end up, or where we are right now, or even where we came from?"

"I guess so. I'm happy with living in my town, playing sports, living with my dad. Should I feel ashamed for living where I do?"

"No, but it isn't as simple as people think. If it was as simple as better housing and better jobs and schools in Providence, why hasn't the government stepped in? Spend money and solve the problem, right? So, tell me why Cranston Street is still a hell hole?"

"I don't know."

"So why would anyone choose to live in a hell hole if they had a way out of it?"

"It doesn't seem like anyone would."

"Did God give you a choice where you ended up being born?"

I put the warm beer bottle on the floor and tried to twist off the bottle cap of the cold one. It wouldn't budge so I set the cold beer down next to the warm beer and sat on the couch while my head spun.

"I don't know what God knows."

"The Lord work in mysterious ways, ain't that right, Tim?"

I still didn't have anything to say.

"I always wonder why God put me in Providence, why he put the rest of us in Providence. Maybe even why you got born in West Beaumont. It's not like any one of us had a say in the matter. You were born there."

She kind of nodded her head toward one of the walls and I guess she meant West Beaumont.

"Pele and me and Marcus, my mom, Henry and Ray and Leon, their families, even Raja, we got put on Cranston Street by God. No use fighting the idea of it, even if the answer might be too difficult. Maybe God meant us to end up here. You know, forty years wandering the desert? Do you think God is making us pay for being black?"

"Maybe I don't want to know what God knows or thinks."

We looked at each other in Beauchamp's basement. I wish I had answers, but I was too young or too ignorant to want to think about the questions. The 'what ifs' of our lives seemed easy, but the 'how comes' seemed difficult.

I sat and looked at her for a bit and then asked the question.

"So why all the drugs?"

"What other way is there for some of us? We don't have much, so we find jobs and take care of our families, or we get pregnant and take care of our kids, but then we don't have time to work, so we have to get a welfare check that only pays for the food, but not the medicine, and then we get lucky and find a job, but we have no car to get there, and even if we could, who's going to take care of the kids? Round and round she goes."

She twirled one finger in the air and then leaned over and put her face in her hands and cried painfully. After a bit, she gathered herself and continued.

"And our men. Our men get involved in hoop or football or drugs. The thing is, they just being used, used by the college coaches or the drug dealers. Whoever is using them don't care none that they get killed. There will always be black men to take their place and keep selling poison or entertain them by dunking basketballs or scoring touchdowns or helping coaches get their big shoe contracts. You sit in the stands and you cheer for your heroes on the court or on the field, and they move on or disappear into the streets, and there is another black man to take their place. I think you white folks might call that capitalism."

She kind of laughed when she said capitalism. This bothered me. I liked sports. It was the best thing about my life. I wanted to play pro sports. I was just obtuse enough to not see the truth in that. Sherri must have noticed my reaction.

"I watched you play basketball, Tim. You not that good."

It was like getting slapped.

"Jesus."

"Most men in Providence don't know it, or won't accept it. They being fooled to think they can get out by selling drugs or being athletes. They think they're selling the product and they don't realize that they are the product. Everyone selling something. Either way, they die here. I've seen it. And understand this, Tim, that your white friends and their parents get their drugs from somewhere. Where do you think that would be?"

I knew guys on my football team who did drugs. I guess I never thought about where they came from.

"Thought so. And sports. That ain't a life. Leon most likely come back home when he all used up and he try to find work, but he die here like the rest of us."

I thought about the way Leon played and couldn't believe he wouldn't make pro.

"Leon's good enough."

"Maybe, but the odds aren't in his favor. He might go to college and play ball, but then, everyone else playing ball is good. He probably won't make it. They just find some other black player."

"You don't give him credit. Maybe he is the one that will make it."

"Yeah, the one. And the other thousands like Marcus or Henry or Ray, even Albert?" She said it sarcastically. "They stuck here like I am, like my mom, like Evelyn." Her voice trailed off and she wiped the tears from her eyes with her fists. "Some people take short cuts because they can't see no other way. They sell drugs, and if they live long enough, they might be in charge of others who sell. But they would have to kill to become a player, and there are too many young blacks wanting to be players. They die defending a neighborhood or a street corner, and once again, there are plenty of black boys being taught that's all they can do so that's all they actually try to do. Like some of the dead guys tonight in front of Beauchamp's. Who did they see making it out of Providence? And then there's the drive-bys and good and bad people all get killed the same way. No, we burn in this furnace."

"What about you? You can get out. You're smart and strong. You're beautiful."

It came out without me meaning it to come out. During all of the time with the craziness over the last few days, I still thought she was beautiful. She saw me staring into her eyes and she held me for a moment. Then she let me go.

"And wouldn't that be a lovely cliché? *White boy comes to Providence and falls in love with a black girl while blacks killing each other. Saves the black girl and they move on out.*"

I slid away from her maybe an inch or so, but she noticed, and the spell was broken.

"You falling in love with me, Tim? You going to marry me? You willing to move to Providence to be with me? Take me away?"

I sat motionless on the couch for what seemed like a very long time. The silence was vast as Sherri kept looking at me. I turned my eyes away and told her the truth.

"No."

"Then put that fantasy away on the shelf where it belong. I ain't falling in love with you. You pretty, but you like this shallow puddle. It spreads out, but eventually the heat of Cranston Street evaporate it and there's nothing left. You a puddle, Tim."

I knew she was right. I finally understood things. I had made my choice already, and I would do it again, if I could move the hour glass back in time. If I could have made it to the bus station yesterday, I would have been gone and home in two hours and playing ball with my friends in three. All of it was true and I was ashamed. I was a puddle. I would haul my ass back to West Beaumont and this would just be a fun story to tell my friends.

"Don't worry, Tim. I don't resent you for it. You got born into your life and I got born into mine. Just don't think it is as simple as black people just moving on out." She took one of the end cushions from the couch and plumped it up. "Sleep on the other couch."

I sat for a minute and stared at her as she closed her eyes purposefully, and I knew she was done talking. I got up and walked over to the light switch and turned it off. I groped my way to the couch where I was going to sleep. The basement was engulfed in complete, utter darkness, and maybe so was I. I lay back and grabbed for an end cushion and stuck it behind my head and tried to sleep. I slept restlessly if I slept at all. I was lost in the nightmare that I knew I could escape, if only I could help black people kill each other.

# Chapter 21

## New Clothes

I woke up with a stiff neck and a knot in my back. The light was on now and Sherri was already up. She paced the floor as I threw my feet over the side of the couch. She had said a lot last night. I wondered if I was too much of a boy to be transformed by it.

"Did you sleep?" I looked at her carefully. I didn't want to have to think any more about the things she said last night.

"I slept." She yawned.

"I think I slept. Usually I dream when I sleep, and I don't remember any dreams."

I stretched my arms and legs and tried to release the knot in my lower back.

"You probably did." Sherri kept pacing. "You tossed and turned enough."

She sat down and folded her hands and dropped her chin to her chest like she was praying. I don't know if she was or not, but I found myself sitting on the couch and I thought that maybe I should be praying, too.

I heard a noise and the floor boards began to move. Beauchamp's feet stepped down the ladder. He was holding two clothes hangers, one with a black suit and a white shirt and the other with two dresses. He carried two boxes under his arm. He opened one up and there were two pair of women's shoes along with an elegant grey purse with black stitching. He handed me the other box. In it was a pair of polished wing-tip shoes.

"Wear this." He handed me the black suit along with the shoes. "Go try it on over by the bar where Sherri can't see you."

He handed me the suit and the white shirt and the shoes, and I went back by the bar where I could be kind of out of Sherri's vision. I tried them on. Everything fit me perfectly, like I had bought the suit and the shirt and the shoes myself. There was a beer bottle left out from the night before. I looked at my reflection on the silver label. I think I looked pretty good. It wasn't the right time for me to think I looked pretty good.

When I came back around, Beauchamp had his back turned to Sherri so she could change. She had picked out a black dress and a wide, black hat. She wore black heels that made her taller than me. She took her hands and smoothed the dress out a bit and looked at her heels and kind of pivoted on one toe to see them better. I found myself staring again. She smiled at me quickly and then looked at Beauchamp.

"I don't understand."

Sherri adjusted her hat and smoothed her dress once more.

"That's one of my wife's dresses. It fits you. I thought it might."

Beauchamp stepped back a bit. Sherri looked at him for a few seconds and then moved close and kissed him gently on the cheek. He almost moved his hands up to her hips, but let them hang by his sides, but he did smile at her. He didn't seem self-conscious about his tobacco-stained teeth because he smiled full and deep and I wondered if that was the first time he had smiled that way in a while.

"I believe you doing us a real kindness, Beauchamp."

"Please. Call me Jean. That's my first name."

"Jean Beauchamp. I like your first name."

Beauchamp kind of blushed and then turned to me.

"You ready?"

I might have looked good in the suit, but I was shaking on the inside.

"Do I have a choice?"

"Listen, so you are in this now. Be brave and be a man and help these coloreds…help these people today. I think you might have it in you."

"Why do you think so?"

"Just do."

Beauchamp moved over to a small closet near the bar. He opened it and pulled down a string that illuminated what was inside. He had some winter clothes hanging from hooks on the wall. On the top shelf of the closet, he pulled down an old box. It said, "U.S. Marines." He opened it up and pulled out a vintage handgun. It gleamed in the light of the closet, like he had been taking care of it since he come back from Korea. It was polished and I could see no evidence of rust. He took it and held it out to me. From one of the clothes hooks, he pulled off a leather holster with a shoulder strap.

"Take off your coat and put this on." I took off my coat and Beauchamp slid the holster over my shoulder. He stuck the gun into the place where the gun was supposed to fit. He put the coat back on me and I could hardly tell there was a holster and a gun underneath.

"I never held a gun before."

"Just in case."

"I can't kill anyone."

"I used to think that about myself, once." He paused for a moment and looked at me some more. "Again, just in case."

I felt the shoulder holster against the side of my chest. Nothing about it felt right. It might have fit me fine, snug and hardly able to be seen under my suit coat, but it didn't fit me, at all. I took the gun out of its holster and handed it back carefully to Beauchamp. He looked at me some more and then carefully took the shoulder holster off of me. He took it and folded it perfectly and hung the holster on the hook on the wall and placed the gun back into the

U.S. Marines box. I let out a deep breath and felt my blood pressure ease. I didn't want the gun. I just didn't.

As he leaned back into the closet, I could see a long rifle standing against the wall. Beauchamp carefully moved some clothes aside and pulled it out. It was very long and there was a scope on top.

"I was a marksman. When I came back from Korea, I swore to my wife that I would never use a gun in anger again."

He showed it to me. It looked like it had been tended to as much as the handgun that now rested back in the U.S. Marines box. It had a polished wood butt and the metallic, silver barrel gleamed. There was what looked like cherry wood along the bottom of the barrel.

"That's a sighting mechanism where you adjust it for distance and elevation and wind speed."

He held the rifle in the crook of his arm. I tried to imagine Beauchamp in a foxhole, aiming his rifle at some distant Chinese soldier who probably didn't want to be in Korea any more than Beauchamp did. He looked at the rifle for a bit, then moved the clothes out of the way and put the rifle back up against the wall. He turned off the light and closed the door and then looked over to Sherri.

"Your brother will be here soon."

I could see Sherri tense when Beauchamp told her this. She was part of the trap for Raja as much as I was. I hated this and how we were all stuck in this situation. It probably wasn't the same, but it seemed almost like Beauchamp and his colored friend in the foxhole. They might have signed up to fight, but back then, Beauchamp and his buddy were probably just in a foxhole trying to save each other. Maybe that is what all of us were really doing.

I snapped out of the thought and remembered why we were going to the funeral in the first place. I hadn't gotten to know Evelyn. The only thing I knew about her was, except for the time she and Sherri watched us play basketball, was that she always seemed scared. It was like whatever awful things Sherri and Marcus and Leon and Henry and Ray, and Beauchamp, and my Meme and Poppy, even Pele and his boys, whatever was happening on Cranston Street, they seemed to accept and deal with in their own way with an outward façade of courage. Evelyn never looked like that. She trembled visibly the night Pele confronted us in front of my grandparent's duplex, and she ran in fear when she came down Cranston Street with Raja's engine roaring, just before her life came to an end and she didn't have to fear anything anymore.

We heard a knock on the door.

"That will be Marcus. He said he and his friends would sneak by to pick you up, Sherri. He said Tim should wait about an hour before leaving my duplex and walk directly down Cranston Street. Marcus seemed to think that Raja's people wouldn't be anywhere else but near the church, so you'll be safe until then."

Beauchamp turned to Sherri. He put out both hands and held on to hers. He was no longer hideous nor was he disgusting, and when he smiled, it seemed like his face and teeth were exactly the way they were supposed to be.

"I'm scared for you." He held firmly onto her hands.

"I know you are."

"I've only just gotten to know you."

"I'm not dying today, Jean. None of us are."

She continued to hold his hands and then turned to look at me.

"You don't deserve to be here, Tim."

"You don't deserve to be here, either."

"God chose me and you and Jean for this place at this time."

She smiled at me and gave me a gentle kiss. She moved away from us and began to climb the ladder in her beautiful dress and hat and heels, holding carefully onto her grey purse. Beauchamp moved me and himself away so Sherri wouldn't be embarrassed while climbing the steps. That's something a father would have done to protect his daughter, I think.

Just before she reached the top, we could hear her say, "Yea, though I walk through the shadow of death." She disappeared through the opening in the floorboards and we could hear her open the back door in Beauchamp's kitchen. We heard her heels click down the steps and then there was silence. She was now with Marcus and Leon and Henry and Ray on their way to Evelyn's service and an unavoidable collision with Raja. I didn't say good bye to her because I couldn't, or maybe I just wasn't ready to.

# Chapter 22

## Filling a Void

Whatever air was in the basement had long since been replaced by a vacuum that Sherri had left behind. I know I felt it and maybe Beauchamp felt it too, because he stood there looking up through the opening for a very long time. Finally, he turned to me.

"Now, you wait. Marcus said for you to leave through my front door and walk right down Cranston Street and turn left toward the bus station. The church is just a little ways down on the left. The main entrance to the church is around back, where the parking lot is."

"What happens then?"

"You trust Pele."

I thought about how much he had scared me the two times I met him, but somehow, knowing what I knew about him and his past and Sherri and Marcus, there was no way for me to get home without his help. I kind of bent over and put my hands on my knees, like the little strength I had left was ebbing and I might not be able to even climb the steps of Beauchamp's ladder.

"Try to be brave, Tim. We can go upstairs now." Beauchamp climbed up the stairs and I followed. The kitchen had been swept of glass shards and I could see where Beauchamp had worked on the dry wall. The bullet holes were covered over by new plaster. He must have been very busy last night. I followed him into his living room. Most of the art had been taken down, and he must have replaced one of the windows because I could see a new sash around it. He had covered his couches and rocking chair with plastic and a ladder stood in the middle of the room with a paint can and brush sitting on the top step. The floor was covered with tarp.

"I had to start to fix this," he said as he gestured around his room.

"Where are the two pictures? The one of you in the marines and you and your wife?"

He stood for a moment and looked around the room and then settled his eyes on mine.

"They're gone."

He stared at me and I realized that those precious pictures of his had not survived the gun fire from the night before.

"Don't worry. This home is what I need to protect and the memories in it. The pictures were just glass, and they weren't alive anymore. It's this house that's alive."

We stood in his living room for quite a while without talking. I watched the hands move on Beauchamp's numberless clock. Finally, it was time. He reached out his three-fingered hand and I took it.

"You'll get through this."

I shook his hand again and smiled a little bit and walked to his front door. I opened it without looking back and stepped carefully over his front porch. It was still a mess from last night's war. It didn't seem that the outside of his porch was what needed fixing. It was what was inside that mattered to Beauchamp.

I stepped down his stairs and looked to my right. My Meme and Poppy's duplex sat undisturbed. I walked up the staircase, that was completely fixed from the drive by, and knocked on the door. I waited a moment and knocked again. No one answered and I figured that Meme and Poppy had already gone to Evelyn's funeral. I felt like a very small person that I wouldn't be able to see them before the service, like that was something I really needed to do. I pressed my face up against the front window of their duplex, half expecting to see both of them sitting on their threadbare couch. Their duplex was as empty as I felt. I walked off the porch, and taking a deep breath, headed toward the end of Cranston Street. Buses drove by and cars honked, but I didn't really notice. Life in Providence carried on, but there was a young woman being laid out at a church nearby and none of the sounds or the people or the smells or the sights registered at all.

I got to the end of Cranston Street and turned left. I walked for a few minutes until I drew even with the bus station. It was busy for a Thursday morning, I guess. Buses pulled in and out and taxis dropped off and picked up and no one seemed to notice me. I walked another minute or two. I could see a long line of people snaking out onto the street and around to the main entrance to the church in the back. There must have been hundreds of people coming to pay their respects to Evelyn's parents and say their goodbyes. I joined the end of the line and slowly made my way forward in a sea of black faces.

It was another broiling day in Providence. I could feel the sweat begin to soak through my white shirt and the suitcoat began to chafe my armpits. I kept my head down as much as I could while still trying to see in front of me. Many of the black men mopped their brows with handkerchiefs while the woman tried to cool themselves with ornate fans. People wept and there was an occasional wail. The line continued to move slowly and relentlessly until finally, I was in the parking lot, not very far from the main door of the church. I didn't think I had much courage left, but somehow, I kept moving forward, inexorably, toward whatever waited in store for me in the parking lot behind that church. That's when I felt a hand on my shoulder. I turned and there was Pele, all in black. He wore a black fedora and black button-down shirt with a black tie. His black suitcoat hung off his shoulders perfectly. He had black pants that tapered down to pointy black boots that had gold tips on the toes. He had expensive sunglasses that framed his head. The total blackness of his outfit did nothing to help him blend in, though. People looked at him and murmured and there was a palpable tension to the crowd.

"Just walk. Don't look around."

He guided me with his hand on the small of my back and we

neared the steps leading up and into the church. I looked in front of me and I recognized at each side of the door some of Pele's henchmen. To my left there was a circle of men and women. I saw Ray with his hands folded and hanging down by his waist. To my right I saw Marcus with a hat on, probably to keep his extraordinary afro in check. To his left stood Henry. He wore no suitcoat and his arms hung down as long as ever. Sweat began to course down my face as the heat became unbearable, to the point where I felt faint like I was going down. Just then, the sun disappeared. I felt a hand on my other shoulder. Leon's massiveness once again blotted out the sun.

"I be yo bodyguard today."

He said it so only I could hear him. His voice was a vibration meant only for me. I wish I felt comforted, but I didn't. I couldn't see how his massiveness could stop one of Raja's bullets.

We continued our procession until we reached the bottom stair leading up into the church. Men and women and children flowed in and out. It was a terrible scene, regardless of whether Raja was anywhere near. Sudden death in the city. *I shall come as a thief in the night.* Just then, I looked up and saw Sherri walking out of the church. Everyone saw her and a heavy silence fell upon the crowd. No one cried or wailed or spoke. As she took her first step down the long church staircase, a dark, threatening car rolled into the parking lot and came to a stop not twenty feet from the stairs leading up to the church. All four doors opened. Three men stepped out from the back seat. A fourth came around from the driver's side front door and walked quickly around the front of the car and opened the front passenger door. A small black man in a dark grey suit and pearl-white hat stepped out from the car. I wasn't breathing, and I think no one else at the church at that moment was breathing either. A deathly quiet settled over everyone who stood in line or waited on the steps. This had to be Raja. He was dwarfed by the other four men who now lined up, shoulder to shoulder, a few paces behind.

"I here to pay my respects."

His voice was high, like a child's. He had three rings on his right hand and two rings on his left. He took a step closer to the church. The crowd on the staircase parted and Sherri walked down toward Raja. She was tall, and her face held firm as she got to the bottom step, not ten feet from where Raja stood. He put his hands by his side and spoke in a clear, child-like voice that made me shiver. Its seeming innocence was displaced by the pure evil of his visage. He looked at Sherri, up and down, like he was surveying a piece of property he wanted and was going to take. No one moved. The sounds of Providence disappeared as the heat of the day reached its zenith.

"Shouldn't have been nowhere near when we drive by."

"But I was."

"Can't let that pass. You has to go."

He smiled when he said it. It was the smile of a shark. His teeth were brilliantly white, but they stood in stark contrast to what I could see from where I stood. None of them were straight. They angled severely in twisted deformity. One of his front teeth stuck out prominently. When his smile disappeared, the ugly tooth remained clearly visible, protruding through his lips. It made his face hideous. Pele stood next to me, still hidden from Raja and his men. He took his hand away from the small of my back and reached slowly around to the deep part of his suitcoat. I looked over and a silver handgun was now in his hands, hidden by his pant leg. I felt Leon slide a bit in front of me. I wanted to wipe the sweat off of my brow, but I was paralyzed.

"She did nothing to you, Raja. She didn't need to die."

Sherri held her black purse on her left side with her left hand. I saw her hand tremble as she spoke.

"Cranston Street mine."

A breeze kicked up and some baked dust from the parking lot

swirled to create a ruinous vortex. Sherri took her purse and carefully moved it to the front of her dress.

"You just in the way." His lips parted and the rest of his hateful teeth reemerged.

Sherri slowly reached with her right hand and opened up her purse and pulled out a small handgun and pointed it directly at Raja's eyes. She pulled back the hammer of the gun. She was crying now, but her right hand was steady, and the gun remained motionless. I could see the small muscles in her right hand begin to flex, putting pressure on the inevitable trigger.

"Not anymore."

A crack rang out and at the same instant, Raja's eyes widened, blood forming within the outline of his deformed teeth. His body remained erect for a moment, with a look of confusion and astonishment, and then, it slowly crumbled to the ground, face first, teeth jamming into the hard, broken asphalt. In the same instant, almost on cue, Pele raised his gun and shot the guy who had opened the door for Raja. He doubled over and went down like a stone. The three other men who had come with Raja all went down as well, one at a time, like someone was target shooting. No one screamed or ran or looked even remotely surprised. Pele put the gun into his coat pocket and nonchalantly walked toward the back of the parking lot where a silver car sat. He stepped over Raja, catching his toe imperceptibly on the back of the dead man's head, jarring it slightly. Three of Pele's men walked out from within the crowd. They stepped deliberately, opening the doors of the silver car and closing them in unison. At that moment, I looked up and caught the glint of something shiny from on top of one of the tenements. A man moved away from the edge of the building and disappeared on the other side of the roof. He seemed to be carrying something long in the crook of his arm, but it was hard for me to see what it was. I looked back to the silver car. It started up and moved easily and peacefully through the crowd that parted for it. With its engine purring quietly, the car exited the parking lot. Still, no one moved.

The silver car turned right and drove by the bus station, and then turned right again and moved smoothly down Cranston Street, like a shark in shallow water, swimming patiently, knowing it's on the top of the food chain and its next meal is only moments away. Coming from the other side of Providence, a scream of police cars, sirens wailing, flew into the parking lot. Gravel and broken pieces of asphalt and baked dust pulsed out from behind. It couldn't have been more than a minute from when Raja was killed. I was surprised at the speed in which they responded. They had to have been close by. Police officers jumped out of their cars with their weapons drawn. The head police officer in the main car moved toward Sherri, stepping over one of Raja's dead buddies. She no longer had the gun in her hand. It had disappeared. The police officer screamed at her.

"Who killed these men?"

Sheri said nothing. No one said anything. Everyone just glared at the police.

"No one saw who killed these men? No one? Not you?"

He stepped right up to where Sherri remained standing.

"Some men, they gone now. Drove off in a red car."

The police officer looked closely at Sherri. She didn't twitch a muscle.

"Anyone know anything at all? No? Ok, no one leaves until we get some answers."

I could see how he was trying to look frustrated, but it came off as being almost theatrical, like the police knew something and what they were doing was all part of an elaborate play. Leon moved in front of me some more. Maybe he didn't want the cops to see some white kid at a black person's funeral near the projects of Cranston Street. As we inched toward where the police were rounding everyone up for questioning, I glanced to my right.

Quickly, almost unperceptively, the gun that Sherri had pointed at Raja's eyes moved back from one person to the next, heading in the opposite direction of the police and disappearing toward the back of the crowd.

"No one's leaving until we get statements from all of you. No one."

His voice was lowered now. He seemed to know that no one was going to tell him anything. The cops began to gather folks toward the police cars. I stayed hidden behind Leon who moved with the crowd, but at the last moment, he turned me toward a side door of the church that was slightly ajar. He opened the door for me and kind of nudged me inside and then turned to keep me from being seen by the police. Meme and Poppy waited there for me.

"Let's go, Timothy. We're leaving out the front of the church. We'll walk home on Cranston Street."

I was too shocked to say anything. What I realized at that moment was that whatever just happened, my grandparents were in on it. We moved quickly through the cool of the basement of the church. We walked up a flight of stairs and entered the foyer. I recognized one of Pele's guys waiting there. He was dressed in a black suit, just like Pele, but no hat. He opened the door for the three of us. He looked out to make sure no one untoward was around. After checking for a while, he waved us through the door, and we emerged into the hazy sunshine and broiling heat. We walked down the front steps of the church and turned right. It seemed unusual to me that all the police were in the back parking lot of the church and no one was out front. Shouldn't the place be thick with cops, front and back?

When we got to Cranston Street, we turned right again. Our pace was determined, but not overtly fast. Black faces nodded at Meme and Poppy as they passed us. Others walked along with us, almost forming an assemblage of protection. My Poppy held on to my elbow from one side and my Meme held on to me from the other. The black people kept moving with us, maintaining a perfect cadence with our steps. A silver car drove by slowly, just as we reached Beauchamp's duplex where he rocked on his favorite chair. His porch was shot up but he rocked on his chair like it was just another day. The driver's side window opened, and I could see Pele, his hat and sunglasses still on. He looked at me like he had always looked at me: predator to the prey. His sunglasses slid down from his nose, just a bit, and he looked up and gave a slight, almost imperceptible nod to Beauchamp. Beauchamp's clothes were filthy as I expected them to be when he was outside his home, and he had a huge wad of tobacco in his mouth. He nodded once at Pele and let out a stream of tobacco juice that landed at his feet by his rocker. The stain added to the years of blemish on his shoes. Pele's window rolled back up and his car moved off in the direction of the armory. It stopped at the street light and turned right, disappearing into the shimmering heat. The noises of Providence returned, almost like the heart of the city returned to its constant beat.

# Chapter 23

## Duplicity

When we were in my Meme and Poppy's duplex, I sat heavily onto their threadbare couch. Poppy took off his suitcoat and loosened his tie. He laid his coat on his rocking chair, careful to keep it from wrinkling. He sat down in his chair and looked at me. I was still numb from what happened, so I didn't say anything. Slowly, the tiniest of smiles formed on his face and his eyes twinkled. Meme came in carrying a tray with three glasses and a pitcher of iced tea. Poppy took one of the glasses from the tray and took a small sip. He licked his lips and let out a satisfied, "ah" and sat back comfortably into his rocker. Meme put the tray down on a table that sat in front of the couch. She handed me a glass and she took one for herself and the three of us sat quietly and sipped tea like today was just another warm, lazy afternoon. I waited for them to explain what the hell just happened. The silence was interminable and not being able to take it anymore, I blurted out.

"Jesus, Poppy!"

"Are you referring to your Meme's ice tea, or something else."

"You know what I'm talking about."

Poppy's eyes continued to sparkle. I looked at Meme and her face beamed. After a few moments, my Meme started in.

"We were afraid for you and your friends."

Meme shrugged her shoulders and put down her iced tea. She folded her arms across her chest and breathed in deeply once or twice.

"When Evelyn was killed, it almost broke Cranston Street." Her smile disappeared. "Cranston Street isn't perfect, but there was a sort of balance to the neighborhood. There is so much pain and suffering here, but it was in balance. Then Raja tried to destroy

167

it."

Poppy shifted in his rocking chair. Meme kept on.

"No one likes that Pele is what he is and does what he does. Too many people hurt by the drugs he sells. But he has always been one of ours; a part of Cranston Street. And he kept our peace. We all understood it, even the police. And then Evelyn was killed, and Sherri was being targeted, and you for that matter, so we all came together to put an end to it."

"Actually," Poppy chimed in, "It was Pele's idea, along with Beauchamp's."

"They hate each other," I said, and my confusion grew, but that, of course, was how I had felt ever since I got here.

Meme crossed her ankles and breathed deeply. Her glasses rose and fell on her chest, held in place by a black string.

"They do, but Raja couldn't be allowed to take over. Beauchamp called a meeting last night for all of Cranston Street, right here in our duplex. Pele came. Some other folks, too. Beauchamp snuck Sherri and Marcus over after you fell asleep. We argued, but eventually, Sherri decided she had to be the one who killed Raja. Marcus fought her, and especially Beauchamp. He said there was enough bloodshed on Cranston Street, and he didn't want Sherri to be part of it, but she's a strong woman and no one could talk her out of it. I didn't like how you were made to be bait, Tim, but you would have been killed otherwise, and your Poppy and me knew it. It was the only chance. Pele said nothing during the meeting. He just looked at us through his sunglasses. After a while, he took them off. We all could see the years of sadness reflected in his eyes. He looked at everyone there, one at a time, and said he would take care of everything else. Everything."

My Meme kind of lifted her eyebrows up and away from her glasses to emphasize the word everything.

"He got up off the same couch we're sitting on now. He walked out the front door, but before he put his glasses back on, he looked at Sherri and Marcus and nodded. He put his sunglasses high up on his nose and walked out. We couldn't do anything else but trust him, but I don't think he was OK with Sherri killing Raja."

"So, all of Cranston Street was in on the plan."

"Almost everyone. Pele spread the word quickly and so did Marcus and his friends. Pretty soon, the word had been passed. But Beauchamp wasn't part of the plan. He said he'd go along with whatever we decided, but he wanted to be sure that Sherri would be ok, and you. He said whatever the coloreds decided to do to fix the problem was fine by him, but he wanted to be left out of it. That's when he left. We heard him working on his house, fixing it up all night. That home of his is precious to him."

"But I don't think Sherri ever pulled the trigger."

"We stood in the doorway of the church basement, waiting for you. We thought for sure Sherri was going to kill Raja. But then Raja was killed, and Sherri still held the gun in front of her. The hammer of the gun was still cocked when Raja crumpled to the ground. We were stunned just like she was, just like you, probably."

"Beauchamp killed Raja, didn't he?"

I looked first at my Meme and then at Poppy.

"That's what we figured. I don't think Beauchamp could let Sherri pull the trigger. She certainly seemed like she was about to."

Poppy took another sip of his iced tea, and once again let out an "ah."

"That damned Beauchamp."

"Yeah, that damned Beauchamp," I said, and I took another sip of tea.

Finally, I could hear the noises of Cranston Street as people talked and music blared, and buses moved up and down the street like they always seemed to do.

# Chapter 24

## Broken Laces

I took an outlet pass from Henry and drove to the basket. Marcus raced down the right sideline and Ray down the left. I did a cross-over dribble and left my defender grasping at nothing. Two more guys tried to stop me. I head faked like I was going to shoot. The two guys jumped up to try to swat away my shot, but instead of shooting, I adjusted my body and lobbed a pass high into the evening. That's when Leon's enormous body leaped toward the heavens as he raced down the center of the court, trailing slightly behind me. He corralled the ball with one hand and then with one, massive, powerful sweep, he slammed the ball through the chain-link netting of the hoop. The force of it rocked the metal pole. It swung back and forth, somehow holding onto the concrete that bucked at the notion. He hung from the rim with both of his massive hands, pulling his feet high up, biceps straining under his skin, and let out another bellowing "Ah!" He landed back to earth, gathered himself, and ran back on defense. He thumped his chest hard and continued to scream out "Ah!" as the crowd around the court and on the bleachers whooped. Leon ran up to me and gave me a flying chest bump. He crashed into me hard enough that I lost my balance and went careening across the court. Somehow, I managed to put one hand down to keep me from falling. I scurried back up and yelled out my own "Ah!" and the game continued in the heat, and old men with fat bellies and young women in skimpy summer dresses and mothers with their kids in strollers and a bunch of cops and the ice-cream guy who parked his ice cream truck nearby, and the mailman and a couple soldiers from the armory, and young shirtless boys with shorts that hung off their hips, bare foot or wearing basketball shoes with worn out toes and knotted laces, everyone celebrated the joy of their nighttime game.

Pele sat on the top bench, a wad of twenties in his hand, keeping up his nightly hustle while some of his boys ran his corners and continued to sell his poison. Finally, the game ended, and high fives and fists bumps were exchanged, and I found myself once again sitting with Marcus and Leon and Henry and Ray and Sherri. Everyone took off their shirts, except for Sherri, who wore a beautiful, floral blouse and tight shorts that showed all of her long legs and of course, her skinny ankles. Our bodies glistened with sweat in the deep heat.

Pele finished collecting his money (I think he bet on us this time) and stepped off the bleachers with his crew. He was in his usual, all-black outfit. He wore the same black hat with the big, gold "P" on front. He strode confidently toward us, like a snake preparing to eat its prey. His crew stood behind him in their usual protective formation. None of their faces showed any expression, and almost in unison, they folded their arms across their chest. A few days ago, I was terrified by the gesture.

"You won me money tonight."

He looked from one of us to the next.

"'Bout time we did something for you."

Marcus stood up and his team stood up and so did I and so did Sherri.

"Think any more about what I asked?"

He took his hand and slid his dark sunglasses off his nose and stared at Sherri. His mouth moved just a bit, like maybe he was smiling.

"I'm still nobody's woman."

Sherri stepped away from us and moved closer to Pele. She leaned forward and put both her hands on his chest. She kissed him gently, first on his right cheek and then his left. She took her hands off his chest and took a step back toward us.

"That fo sure."

His snake-like mouth showed the slightest bit of a smile. Then he put back on his dark sunglasses. He gave a nod with his head and he turned and strode off with his entourage in tow. I watched them walk out through the rusted gate of the court and slowly disappear into the night. I found myself letting out my breath that I must have been holding, but this time, I wasn't holding it in because I was petrified, like I was a few nights back. Something important and profound had just happened, and I was glad to be part of whatever it was.

"When you leaving?"

Marcus sat back down and so did the rest of us. Sherri sat close to her brother.

"My Meme and Poppy are walking me to the bus station, first thing in the morning. I think I've violated your personal space for long enough."

"Haw!" laughed Leon.

"You the whitest white boy I ever know."

Ray fell off the bleachers again and Henry bent over and slapped the broken, dirty concrete of the court with both of his palms. He let out a howl and then rolled over with Ray and they began a fake wrestling match. Marcus smiled widely. He wore the same red head band he did when I first met him a lifetime ago.

"So, you going back to West Beaumont? Leave this all behind?"

Marcus gestured dramatically with his hand and presented the panorama of Cranston Street.

"I think it's time."

I reached over and opened my gym bag. I pulled out my walking around sneakers. I unlaced my almost perfectly white Converse All-Stars with the blue and gold intertwined laces. I carefully pulled them off and placed them on the bench between Marcus and me. I put on my other sneakers and tied them up and sat for a bit and let the noises of Cranston Street settle over us like a comfortable blanket. Then I picked up my Converse All-Stars, and after looking at them for a few seconds, I handed them to Marcus. Cranston Street became very quiet as Marcus took them in his hands. He looked at them for a few seconds, and then he looked at Ray and Henry who had stopped wrestling, and then at the enormous form of Leon, and then at his beautiful sister who sat with a glow that almost always seemed to shimmer around her. He bent over and unlaced his worn out, almost no toes, ripped at the seams, black sneakers with the laces that seemed like they might break at any moment. He held them up to me. I reached out and took them and carefully placed them into the deepest part of my gym bag. We stood up, quietly in the darkness, and looked at each other, really, for the first time.

"You think you can make it back to your Meme and Poppy's duplex by yourself, white boy?"

"I think I can."

I stood up and looked deeply into the eyes of first Sherri, then Ray, then Leon and Henry, and finally Marcus. They held me in their translucent, astonishing, curiously glorious eyes. I picked up my gym bag, and without saying goodbye, turned and walked out of the gate and headed toward my grandparent's duplex. I smelled barbeque and cheap wine and diesel from buses that moved this way and that, and I heard Ray Charles and Aretha Franklin streaming from cars that drove nearby, and I saw groups of men and women leaning on picnic tables, focused in muffled conversation. I walked across the hot, broken pavement and up my grandparent's front porch and opened the front door and stepped inside and Providence hummed and breathed, and the heavens shined over the entire length of Cranston Street like the street lights there were never broken.

# Chapter 25

## That Damn Beauchamp

The next morning, my grandparents and I left their duplex on our way to them seeing me off at the bus station. We passed Beauchamp's duplex and stopped. Of course, he was there, but this time, he wore clean clothes and decent shoes and the tobacco spit that stained his porch had been scrubbed away. There were still some bullet holes along the frame of his porch. He must have been hard at work fixing up the remaining damaged part of his home. I thought it looked sturdy enough to remain intact.

"Am I going to see you again?"

"I think I'll be back again, next summer."

"Maybe it won't be so hot."

He grabbed at his shirt collar and gave it a tug, like he was letting out the heat that had accumulated under his shirt over the course of the morning.

"Probably not."

I smiled at him and gave him a quick nod. He grinned and I could see his tarnished teeth, but they didn't seem particularly green in the new, early-morning light.

My Meme and Poppy walked with me down Cranston Street, quietly, and I let the orchestra of the city wash over me, like I was being cleaned a little bit by its symphony. We turned, and I left Cranston Street behind. We walked along peacefully, and in a bit, we arrived at the bus station. It was quite busy. People were coming into Providence or leaving it, just like me.

"We're glad you were here with us this week, Timothy."

My Poppy shook my hand and handed me my suitcase and gym bag. My Meme stepped close to me and pulled me in tightly and hugged me for a very long time. She stepped back and I could see she had tears in her eyes, behind her glasses with the black string attached so she wouldn't lose them.

"Yes. I had a good week."

The three of us stood there next to a silver bus that held its door open for me, ready to transport me back to West Beaumont.

"Can you call and ask my dad if he can pick me up at the bus station? He'll be wondering why I'm coming home a day early."

"We already did. He'll be waiting when you get there."

I didn't know what else to say so I turned and started to climb the stairs of the silver bus.

"I almost forgot."

My Meme put her foot on the bottom stair of the bus and handed me a large, brown paper bag with twine handles. I took it from her and looked inside. My red, white, and blue Julius Irving autographed ABA basketball nestled inside. I looked at her quizzically.

"I don't understand."

"It wasn't us. It was that damned Beauchamp."

Poppy smiled this time when he said the name. I smiled at both of them and I told them I loved them very much and would be back next summer to spend another week with them. I took the bag and climbed up the stairs and I walked to the back of the bus and sat by myself. The air brakes hissed, and the bus backed out of the station. I looked out my tinted window that I was sure my grandparents could not see through. They waved goodbye to the bus and stood there and watched its long, sleek frame pull out of the station. I had a hard time turning away from them as the bus rolled past Cranston Street. As the bus made its wide turn, I looked out the window once more. Pele and his boys stood on the corner, looking fierce in the morning heat.

The bus yielded for traffic coming and going from the Civic Center, before it turned on to Route 95. In just a few minutes, the bus crossed over the Rhode Island/Massachusetts state line and headed north, back toward where I lived.

There weren't many people on the bus, so I had the back to myself. I sat a few seats away from the restroom at the far end of the bus, but I was close enough that I could tell that it needed to get changed out. The smell reminded me of urine from outside my grandparents' duplex, but it didn't bother me so much now. Still, I decided I wasn't going to use the bathroom, no matter how much I might need to pee on my way home.

I reached down and pulled out the ABA basketball Beauchamp had retrieved for me. I'm not sure he knew it was missing, but he must have noticed something because here it was in my hand. It was a comfort for me as I held it with both of my hands. Maybe he knew I needed it with me before I could leave Cranston Street.

I put the ball back into the bag. I reached over and opened my gym bag. I had placed it on its own seat next to me. I dug deep and pulled out the worn basketball shoes Marcus had given me last night. I ran my fingers along the sides where the stitching was busting out and then to the toes, to the place where the rubber met the canvas and it was just about torn apart. I looked carefully at the places where Marcus had restrung the laces, one knot after another where they had broken and Marcus had to save them. I understood that the laces would snap again, once I wore them in my next basketball game, so I worked hard to untie them and tried to redo the knots so the laces would hold out. I worked purposefully at repairing the laces and saving the basketball shoes, not realizing how much time and distance had passed.

I felt the bus slow and looked up and realized that the bus had turned off Route 93 and was pulling into the bus station in West Beaumont. I looked at the old, black hoop shoes and decided that the laces were sufficiently rebuilt and would hold up whenever I decided to wear them. The bus pulled into the station and the air brakes hissed and people slowly walked down the aisle to disembark. I was the last one to leave. I made sure I had everything before I walked down the stairs and stepped into the clean air and earthy smells of West Beaumont. Across the parking lot, my dad leaned against our big-ass, Ford Fairlane. His arms were folded when I got off the bus, and he waited for me to cover the distance. I put down my suitcase and gym bag and ABA basketball and hugged my dad. He tried to let go of me, but I pulled him in harder and held the hug as people walked this way and that.

"So, the week went well?" he asked as our hug finally ended.

"Was it what you expected?"

I looked at him and shook my head and the two of us got into our car and drove away. Our house was about five miles from the bus station, and neither one of us spoke. It was a loud silence, but a good silence where I think I knew that whatever I had experienced on Cranston Street, my dad would give me the time to process it and soon, I would be able to tell him everything. Right now, not speaking with me was a wonderful gift. He could have pressed me for details, but he loved me enough to let me work things out for myself, whatever it was that I experienced over the last week in Providence. I looked at him as we drove toward our home, his left elbow leaning on the driver's side door, the window open and fresh, clean air blowing in. We drove carefully past the high school and the beige-colored, perfect basketball court. People I didn't know ran up and down the court, their expensive, clean basketball shoes gleaming in the sunshine.

# Chapter 26

## Hometown Boys

James and Michael and Joe and Kahlil and me leaned against my big-ass Ford Fairlane late that night. We had played all day and late into the night, ever since I got home from Providence. It was August and it should have been hot, but it had been a pleasant day with a gentle breeze and blue sky that seemed to go on forever. The night was cool. A fresh breeze blew over West Beaumont.

By this time, we had changed into dry t-shirts because we were soaked from playing hoop all day and deep into the night and we kind of stunk.

As usual, we beat just about everyone who dared take us on. We felt that wonderful feeling of complete exhaustion athletes feel after hours of sprinting and jumping, raining jumpers, blocking shots, and throwing behind the back passes. Michael sipped on a beer he had pulled from his cooler. James and Joe drank Gatorade. Kahlil chugged from a cold bottle of water and I sipped from a can of some ice-cold Coca Cola.

"So, did you have a good time in Providence?" Michael grabbed another beer from his cooler and took a long swallow.

"Did you get to play with the brothers?" James finished his Gatorade.

"Was it what you expected?" Joe looked at me in the dark.

His bright eyes shined at me. Kahlil looked at me quietly and waited.

"Yes, yes, and no."

The four of them stood in the dark, illuminated only by my car radio that played "What's Going On?" by Marvin Gaye. I could see their faces clearly and knew they were waiting for me to share details. I took my red, white, and blue ABA basketball that sat at my feet, picked it up and spun it on my finger. Kahlil turned toward me and I began to answer their questions in order: "Once in a life time experience, held my own in the games I played in, and nothing like I expected."

"What do you mean?" Joe stood a step closer.

Michael put down his beer. James shifted his weight as he leaned against my car. Kahlil folded his arms.

"I didn't understand much of anything. I didn't understand how my grandparents could stay in that neighborhood."

"Hmm." Joe kind of grunted.

"I thought the black people I met would be just like you two."

I nodded toward Kahlil and Joe. They didn't say anything but continued to look hard at me.

"What made you think that they would be just like us?"

Kahlil unfolded his arms and shifted his weight.

"The guys I met in Providence were black. You two are black."

I shrugged my shoulders.

"But now you realized not all black people are alike?"

"Yes."

"So, what do you think about black people now?"

I looked at my Coke can for a bit and then raised it to my lips, but it was already empty, so I tossed it into Michael's cooler.

"A wise white man I met on Cranston Street said that he would never be able to understand what it means to be a black man. I think I agree. I spent a week in Providence, and I got a peek behind the curtain. But no matter what, a piece of me always knew that I could get on a bus and come back here."

Joe looked at Michael and Kahlil looked at James. There was a thinness to the cool of the night time air as we stood quietly and tried to see each other in the darkness.

"There was always going to be that."

Whatever else I thought I wanted to say or thought I should say was put away for another night, after another basketball game with my friends, when maybe I was mature enough to articulate the swirl of thoughts and emotions and truths and misconceptions. Finally, James broke the silence.

"New basketball shoes?"

Everyone looked down, and even though it was dark, by the light of the radio, they could see I wore black, worn-out hoop shoes with knotted laces and rips along the soles and toes that were almost completely hanging off.

"I like them," I said as I lifted up one hoop shoe. "They fit me well."

I reached down and brushed off some of the dust that had accumulated on them as we stood around my car. The darkness of the night covered us, and we stood quietly and looked across to the basketball court now empty of players.

Rick Collins

# About the Author

Rick Collins is a teacher and coach of thousands of kids from Penacook, New Hampshire, Andover, Massachusetts, West Hartford, Simsbury, and Plainville, Connecticut. He makes his home in Simsbury. He is the loving husband of Betsy Dietlin Collins and their beloved children, Hannah and Sam. He is the author of *It Emptied Us* as well as the upcoming thriller, *A Run on the River*. You can find him on Facebook and twitter at @RickyCollins25.

Made in the USA
Columbia, SC
09 March 2020